D0416845

NOTTINGHAMSHIRE COUNTY COUNCIL
THE
BRUNTS SCHOOL
EDUCATION DEPARTMENT

THE NEW WINDMILL BOOK OF

NINETEENTH CENTURY SHORT STORIES

EDITED BY MIKE HAMLIN,
CHRISTINE HALL AND JANE BROWNE

Heinemann Educational Publishers
Halley Court, Jordan Hill, Oxford OX2 8EJ
Part of Harcourt Education

Heinemann is the registered trademark of Harcourt Educational Limited

First published in the New Windmill Series 1992

03 04 05 06 24 23 22 21 20 19 18

ISBN 0 435 12410 2

British Cataloguing in Publication data for this title
is available from the British Library.

Cover design by Green Street Press
Photograph, The Railway Station (1862)
by W. P. Frith
Courtesy of the Royal Holloway College,
London

The editors and publishers wish to thank the following
for permission to reproduce copyright material:
Country Living by Maupassant: translated by David Coward,
Oxford University Press 1990.
26 Men and A Girl by Maxim Gorky: translated by D. Richards,
Penguin Book of Russian Short Stories. Penguin 1981.

Printed in the UK by Clays Ltd, St Ives plc

Contents

Introduction

Although people have written short stories for hundreds of years, it was not until the nineteenth century that the short story came to be seen as a genre in its own right. Nineteenth-century critics and writers discussed short stories in ways that encouraged readers to think about them as something more than cut-down novels. The subject matter, form and general characteristics of the short story came under close consideration, and by the end of the century the short story as we know it today was a well developed and very popular form in Europe and North America.

Why did the short story develop as a popular form at this particular time? One important factor was the growing popularity of magazines and journals over the course of the century. The technology for printing was improving, and cheap magazines were widely read. Many of the Victorian novels we now think of as single volumes were originally published as serials in magazines. Most of the authors collected here began their writing careers with publications in journals. The reading public had a taste for fiction and the short story was the ideal form for writers who wanted to earn some immediate money and reach a wide audience. As more people were given the chance of receiving basic education, literacy rates improved and more were able to enjoy reading magazines and books.

In the days before television or radio, reading aloud was a much more popular form of entertainment than it is today, and we know that short stories or instalments of serials were often read aloud within families or groups of friends. Because these short stories reached a wide audience they often dealt with themes and issues that were of considerable importance to people's lives. Like popular fiction today, particular types of story – such as romance, mystery, horror or detection – had an especially wide appeal.

In nineteenth-century Europe and America women writers had more difficulty than men getting their work published: Charlotte Brontë, for example, adopted the pen name 'Currer Bell' when submitting her early works to publishers. Nevertheless, there were powerful women writers at work during the nineteenth century, as we hope you will agree after reading the stories of the six women writers represented in this collection.

We have included stories from different cultures; seven are from Britain, six from the United States, one from South Africa, one from Ireland and two are in translation from originals in French and Russian. We have grouped them according to theme to suggest ways of making comparisons between the stories, and to help you think about possible ways of interpreting them, but each of the stories stands alone, and you may well see links or contrasts between stories in different groupings.

We offer a brief introduction to each story because we think that some background information about the author will help you in your reading and thinking. Where particular words have either changed their meanings, or have dropped out of the language altogether we have suggested a modern equivalent at the bottom of the page. Above all though, we have chosen the short stories in this volume not just as good examples of nineteenth century writing but because we think they will be appealing and interesting to readers today. We hope you enjoy them.

Kate Chopin 1854–1904

Kate Chopin was the child of an Irish immigrant father and a French mother from St Louis. Her father died when Kate was very young and she was brought up in an all female household – mother, grandmother and great grandmother, in the American Deep South.

From the time of her marriage in 1870 Kate lived in New Orleans. She read widely, and she especially admired the stories of the French writer Guy de Maupassant, translating a number of his pieces for American publication.

Kate's own writing began after the death of her husband in 1883. She took her work seriously, bravely picking up and extending themes which less confident writers had tended to pass over. She was especially keen to explore the complex experiences of women in relation to men, family life and the wider world. Her writing was often controversial and many of her stories were refused publication during her lifetime. However, her focus on women's experience and the accessibility of her writing style has generated a lot of recent interest in her work. Chopin's short novel *The Awakening* (1899) is now regularly in print, as are several collections of her short stories.

The Unexpected, written in 1895 originally for a magazine readership, is a typical Kate Chopin short story. It is brief, unadorned; and yet in just a few pages it manages to reach deeply into a relationship and pose a number of important questions about female independence, the nature of physical attraction and the pressures of financial insecurity.

The Unexpected

Kate Chopin

When Randall, for a brief absence, left his Dorothea, whom he was to marry after a time, the parting was bitter; the enforced separation seemed to them too cruel an ordeal to bear. The good-bye dragged with lingering kisses and sighs, and more kisses and more clinging till the last wrench came.

He was to return at the close of the month. Daily letters, impassioned and interminable, passed between them.

He did not return at the close of the month; he was delayed by illness. A heavy cold, accompanied by fever, contracted in some unaccountable way, held him to his bed. He hoped it would be over and that he would rejoin her in a week. But this was a stubborn cold, that seemed not to yield to familiar treatment; yet the physician was not discouraged, and promised to have him on his feet in a fortnight.

All this was torture to the impatient Dorothea; and if her parents had permitted, she surely would have hastened to the bedside of her beloved.

For a long interval he could not write himself. One day he seemed better; another day a 'fresh cold' seized him with relentless clutch; and so a second month went by, and Dorothea had reached the limit of her endurance.

Then a tremulous scrawl came from him, saying he would be obliged to pass a season at the south; but he would first revisit his home, if only for a day, to clasp his dearest one to his heart, to appease the hunger for her presence, the craving for her lips that had been devouring him through all the fever and pain of this detestable illness.

Dorothea had read his impassioned letters almost to

tatters. She had sat daily gazing for hours upon his portrait, which showed him to be an almost perfect specimen of youthful health, strength and manly beauty.

She knew he would be altered in appearance – he had prepared her, and had even written that she would hardly know him. She expected to see him ill and wasted; she would not seem shocked; she would not let him see astonishment or pain in her face. She was in a quiver of anticipation, a sensuous fever of expectancy till he came.

She sat beside him on the sofa, for after the first delirious embrace he had been unable to hold himself upon his tottering feet, and had sunk exhausted in a corner of the sofa. He threw his head back upon the cushions and stayed, with closed eyes, panting; all the strength of his body had concentrated in the clasp – the grasp with which he clung to her hand.

She stared at him as one might look upon a curious apparition which inspired wonder and mistrust rather than fear. This was not the man who had gone away from her; the man she loved and had promised to marry. What hideous transformation had he undergone, or what devilish transformation was she undergoing in contemplating him? His skin was waxy and hectic, red upon the cheekbones. His eyes were sunken; his features pinched and prominent; and his clothing hung loosely upon his wasted frame. The lips with which he had kissed her so hungrily, and with which he was kissing her now, were dry and parched, and his breath was feverish and tainted.

At the sight and the touch of him something within her seemed to be shuddering, shrinking, shriveling together, losing all semblance of what had been. She felt as if it was her heart; but it was only her love.

'This is the way my Uncle Archibald went – in a gallop – you know.' He spoke with a certain derision and in little gasps, as if breath were failing him. 'There's no danger of that for me, of course, once I get south; but the doctors won't answer for me if I stay here during the coming fall and winter.'

Then he held her in his arms with what seemed to be a frenzy of passion; a keen and quickened desire beside which his former and healthful transports were tempered and lukewarm by comparison.

'We need not wait, Dorothea,' he whispered. 'We must not put it off. Let the marriage be at once, and you will come with me and be with me. Oh, God! I feel as if I would never let you go; as if I must hold you in my arms forever, night and day, and always!'

She attempted to withdraw from his embrace. She begged him not to think of it, and tried to convince him that it was impossible.

'I would only be a hindrance, Randall. You will come back well and strong; it will be time enough then,' and to herself she was saying: 'never, never, never!' There was a long silence, and he had closed his eyes again.

'For another reason, my Dorothea,' and then he waited again, as one hesitates through shame or through fear, to speak. 'I am quite – almost sure I shall get well; but the strongest of us cannot count upon life. If the worst should come I want you to have all I possess; what fortune I have must be yours, and marriage will make my wish secure. Now I'm getting morbid.' He ended with a laugh that died away in a cough which threatened to wrench the breath from his body, and which brought the attendant, who had waited without, quickly to his side.

Dorothea watched him from the window descend the steps, leaning upon the man's arm, and saw him enter his carriage and fall helpless and exhausted as he had sunk an hour before in the corner of her sofa.

She was glad there was no one present to compel her to speak. She stayed at the window as if dazed, looking fixedly at the spot where the carriage had stood. A clock on the mantel striking the hour finally roused her, and she realized that there would soon be people appearing whom she would be forced to face and speak to.

Fifteen minutes later Dorothea had changed her house gown, had mounted her 'wheel,' and was fleeing as if Death himself pursued her.

She sped along the familiar roadway, seemingly borne on by some force other than mechanical – some unwonted energy – a stubborn impulse that lighted her eyes, set her cheeks aflame, bent her supple body to one purpose – that was, swiftest flight.

How far, and how long did she go? She did not know; she did not care. The country about her grew unfamiliar. She was on a rough, unfrequented road, where the birds in the wayside bushes seemed unafraid. She could perceive no human habitation; an old fallow field, a stretch of wood, great trees bending thick-leaved branches, languidly, and flinging long, inviting shadows aslant the road; the weedy smell of summer; the drone of insects; the sky and the clouds, and the quivering, lambent air. She was alone with nature; her pulses beating in unison with its sensuous throb, as she stopped and stretched herself upon the sward. Every muscle, nerve, fibre abandoned itself to the delicious sensation of rest that overtook and crept tingling through the whole length of her body.

She had never spoken a word after bidding him good-by; but now she seemed disposed to make confidants of the tremulous leaves, or the crawling and hopping insects, or the big sky into which she was staring.

'Never!' she whispered, 'not for all his thousands! Never, never! not for millions!'

Thomas Hardy 1840–1928

Thomas Hardy was born in 1840, the son of a builder in the rural county of Dorset. Although Hardy is sometimes thought of as a self-educated man, in fact he went to Dorchester High School and then went on to train as an architect, spending some time in London. His main interest, though, was in the countryside and people of Wessex – that area of southern England made up of Dorset and its neighbouring counties. In his novels such as *Tess of the D'Urbevilles* (1891) and *Jude the Obscure* (1895) he set out to observe and describe the lives of ordinary people. He wrote about their life and work, about the making and breaking of relationships.

Although Hardy's work is still widely read and enjoyed today, with many film adaptations of his novels, his writing was poorly received in its day. The novel *Jude the Obscure* was viciously attacked as 'immoral' making Hardy comment, 'The experience completely cured me of further interest in novel writing.' He stopped writing novels in 1895 but continued writing poetry until his death in 1928.

Tony Kytes, the Arch-Deceiver is taken from *Life's Little Ironies* (1895). A group of people on a carrier van take it in turns to tell a story about someone they know to John Lackland, who is returning to the village after an absence of 35 years. In this story the carrier, Mr Burton, tells in colourful Wessex dialect, of what happens to Tony Kytes, a young man who is about to be engaged to Milly.

Tony Kytes, the Arch-Deceiver

Thomas Hardy

I shall never forget Tony's face. 'Twas a little, round, firm, tight face, with a seam here and there left by the smallpox, but not enough to hurt his looks in a woman's eye, though he'd had it badish when he was a boy. So very serious looking and unsmiling 'a was, that young man, that it really seemed as if he couldn't laugh at all without great pain to his conscience. He looked very hard at a small speck in your eye when talking to 'ee. And there was no more sign of a whisker or beard on Tony Kytes's face than on the palm of my hand. He used to sing 'The Tailor's Breeches' with a religious manner, as if it were a hymn:

'O the petticoats went off, and the breeches went on!'

and all the rest of the scandalous stuff. He was quite the women's favourite, and in return, for their likings he loved 'em in shoals.

But in course of time Tony got fixed down to one in particular, Milly Richards, a nice, light, small, tender little thing; and it was soon said that they were engaged to be married. One Saturday he had been to market to do business for his father, and was driving home the waggon in the afternoon. When he reached the foot of the very hill we shall be going over in ten minutes who should he see waiting for him at the top but Unity Sallet, a handsome girl, one of the young women he'd been very tender toward before he'd got engaged to Milly.

As soon as Tony came up to her she said, 'My dear Tony, will you give me a lift home?'

'That I will, darling,' said Tony. 'You don't suppose I could refuse 'ee?'

She smiled a smile, and up she hopped, and on drove Tony.

'Tony,' she says, in a sort of tender chide, 'why did ye desert me for that other one? In what is she better than I? I should have made 'ee a finer wife, and a more loving one too. 'Tisn't girls that are so easily won at first that are the best. Think how long we've known each other – ever since we were children almost – now haven't we, Tony?'

'Yes, that we have,' says Tony, a-struck with the truth o't.

'And you've never seen anything in me to complain of, have ye, Tony? Now tell the truth to me?'

'I never have, upon my life,' says Tony.

'And – can you say I'm not pretty, Tony? Now look at me!'

He let his eyes light upon her for a long while. 'I really can't,' says he. 'In fact, I never knowed you was so pretty before!'

'Prettier than she?'

What Tony would have said to that nobody knows, for before he could speak, what should he see ahead, over the hedge past the turning, but a feather he knew well – the feather in Milly's hat – she to whom he had been thinking of putting the question as to giving out the banns that very week.

'Unity,' says he, as mild as he could, 'here's Milly coming. Now I shall catch it mightily if she sees 'ee riding here with me; and if you get down she'll be turning the corner in a moment, and, seeing 'ee in the road, she'll know we've been coming on together. Now, dearest Unity, will ye, to avoid all unpleasantness, which I know ye can't bear any more than I, will ye lie down in the back part of the waggon, and let me cover you over with the tarpaulin till Milly has passed? It will all be done in a minute. Do! – and I'll think over what we've said; and perhaps I shall put a loving question to you after all, instead of to Milly. 'Tisn't true that it is all settled between her and me.'

Well, Unity Sallet agreed, and lay down at the back end of the waggon, and Tony covered her over, so that the waggon seemed to be empty but for the loose tarpaulin; and then he drove on to meet Milly.

'My dear Tony!' cries Milly, looking up with a little pout at him as he came near. 'How long you've been coming home! Just as if I didn't live at Upper Longpuddle at all! And I've come to meet you as you asked me to do, and to ride back with you, and talk over our future home – since you asked me, and I promised. But I shouldn't have come else, Mr Tony!'

'Ay, my dear, I did ask 'ee – to be sure I did, now I think of it – but I had quite forgot it. To ride back with me, did you say, dear Milly?'

'Well, of course! What can I do else? Surely you don't want me to walk, now I've come all this way?'

'O no, no! I was thinking you might be going on to town to meet your mother. I saw her there – and she looked as if she might be expecting 'ee.'

'O no; she's just home. She came across the fields, and so got back before you.'

'Ah! I didn't know that,' says Tony. And there was no help for it but to take her up beside him.

They talked on very pleasantly, and looked at the trees, and beasts, and birds, and insects, and at the ploughmen at work in the fields, till presently who should they see looking out of the upper window of a house that stood beside the road they were following, but Hannah Jolliver, another young beauty of the place at that time, and the very first woman that Tony had fallen in love with – before Milly and before Unity, in fact – the one that he had almost arranged to marry instead of Milly. She was a much more dashing girl than Milly Richards, though he'd not thought much of her of late. The house Hannah was looking from was her aunt's.

'My dear Milly – my coming wife, as I may call 'ee,' says Tony in his modest way, and not so loud that Unity could overhear, 'I see a young woman a-looking out of window, who I think may accost me. The fact is, Milly, she had a notion that I was wishing to marry her, and since she's discovered I've promised another, and a prettier than she, I'm rather afeard of her temper if she sees us together. Now, Milly, would you do me a favour – my coming wife, as I may say?'

'Certainly, dearest Tony,' says she.

'Then would ye creep under the empty sacks just here in the front of the waggon, and hide there out of sight till we've passed the house? She hasn't seen us yet. You see, we ought to live in peace and good-will since 'tis almost Christmas, and 'twill prevent angry passions rising, which we always should do.'

'I don't mind, to oblige you, Tony,' Milly said; and though she didn't care much about doing it, she crept under, and crouched down just behind the seat, Unity being snug at the other end. So they drove on till they got near the road-side cottage. Hannah had soon seen him coming, and waited at the window, looking down upon him. She tossed her head a little disdainful and smiled off-hand.

'Well, aren't you going to be civil enough to ask me to ride home with you?' she says, seeing that he was for driving past with a nod and a smile.

'Ah, to be sure! What was I thinking of?' said Tony, in a flutter. 'But you seem as if you was staying at your aunt's?'

'No, I am not,' she said. 'Don't you see I have my bonnet and jacket on? I have only called to see her on my way home. How can you be so stupid, Tony?'

'In that case – ah – of course you must come along wi' me,' says Tony, feeling a dim sort of sweat rising up inside his clothes. And he reined in the horse, and waited till she'd come downstairs, and then helped her up beside him. He drove on again, his face as long as a face that was a round one by nature well could be.

Hannah looked round sideways into his eyes. 'This is nice, isn't it, Tony?' she says. 'I like riding with you.'

Tony looked back into her eyes. 'And I with you,' he said after a while. In short, having considered her, he warmed up, and the more he looked at her the more he liked her, till he couldn't for the life of him think why he had ever said a word about marriage to Milly or Unity while Hannah Jolliver was in question. So they sat a little closer and closer, their feet upon the footboard and their shoulders touching, and Tony thought over and over again how handsome Hannah was. He spoke tenderer and tenderer, and called her 'dear Hannah' in a whisper at last.

'You've settled it with Milly by this time, I suppose,' said she.

'N – no, not exactly.'

'What? How low you talk, Tony.'

'Yes – I've a kind of hoarseness. I said, not exactly.'

'I suppose you mean to?'

'Well, as to that – ' His eyes rested on her face, and hers on his. He wondered how he could have been such a fool as not to follow up Hannah. 'My sweet Hannah!' he bursts out, taking her hand, not being really able to help it, and forgetting Milly and Unity, and all the world besides. 'Settled it? I don't think I have!'

'Hark!' says Hannah.

'What?' says Tony, letting go her hand.

'Surely I heard a sort of little screaming squeak under those sacks? Why, you've been carrying corn, and there's mice in this waggon, I declare!' She began to haul up the tails of her gown.

'Oh no; 'tis the axle,' said Tony in an assuring way. 'It do go like that sometimes in dry weather.'

'Perhaps it was . . . Well, now, to be quite honest, dear Tony, do you like her better than me? Because – because, although I've held off so independent, I'll own at last that I do like 'ee, Tony, to tell the truth; and I wouldn't say no if you asked me – you know what.'

Tony was so won over by this pretty offering mood of a girl who had been quite the reverse (Hannah had a backward way with her at times, if you can mind) that he just glanced behind, and then whispered very soft, 'I haven't quite promised her, and I think I can get out of it, and ask you that question you speak of.'

'Throw over Milly? – all to marry me! How delightful!' broke out Hannah, quite loud, clapping her hands.

At this there was a real squeak – an angry, spiteful squeak, and afterward a long moan, as if something had broke its heart, and a movement of the empty sacks.

'Something's there!' said Hannah, starting up.

'It's nothing, really,' says Tony in a soothing voice, and praying inwardly for a way out of this. 'I wouldn't tell 'ee at first, because I wouldn't frighten 'ee. But, Hannah, I've really a couple of ferrets in a bag under there, for rabbiting, and they quarrel sometimes. I don't wish it knowed, as 'twould be called poaching. Oh, they can't get out, bless 'ee – you are quite safe! And – and – what a fine day it is, isn't it, Hannah, for this time of year? Be you going to market next Saturday? How is your aunt now?' and so on, says Tony, to keep her from talking any more about love in Milly's hearing.

But he found his work cut out for him, and wondering again how he should get out of this ticklish business, he looked about for a chance. Nearing home he saw his father in a field not far off, holding up his hand as if he wished to speak to Tony.

'Would you mind taking the reins for a moment, Hannah,' he said, much relieved, 'while I go and find out what father wants?'

She consented, and away he hastened into the field, only too glad to get breathing time. He found that his father was looking at him with rather a stern eye.

'Come, come, Tony,' says old Mr Kytes, as soon as his son was alongside him, 'this won't do, you know.'

'What?' says Tony.

'Why, if you mean to marry Milly Richards, do it, and there's an end o't. But don't go driving about the country with Jolliver's daughter and making a scandal. I won't have such things done.'

'I only asked her – that is, she asked me, to ride home.'

'She? Why, now, if it had been Milly, 'twould have been quite proper; but you and Hannah Jolliver going about by yourselves – '

'Milly's there too, father.'

'Milly? Where?'

'Under the corn-sacks! Yes, the truth is, father, I've got rather into a nunny-watch, I'm afeard! Unity Sallet is there too – yes, at the other end, under the tarpaulin. All three are in that waggon, and what to do with 'em I know no more than the dead! The best plan is, as I'm thinking, to speak out loud and plain to one of 'em before the rest, and that will settle it; not but what 'twill cause 'em to kick up a bit of a miff, for certain. Now which would you marry, father, if you was in my place?'

'Whichever of 'em did *not* ask to ride with thee.'

'That was Milly, I'm bound to say, as she only mounted by my invitation. But Milly – '

'Then stick to Milly, she's the best . . . But look at that!'

His father pointed toward the waggon. 'She can't hold that horse in. You shouldn't have left the reins in her hands. Run on and take the horse's head, or there'll be some accident to them maids!'

Tony's horse, in fact, in spite of Hannah's tugging at the reins, had started on his way at a brisk walking pace, being very anxious to get back to the stable, for he had had a long day out. Without another word Tony rushed away from his father to overtake the horse.

Now of all things that could have happened to wean him from Milly there was nothing so powerful as his father's recommending her. No; it could not be Milly, after all. Hannah must be the one, since he could not marry all three as he longed to do. This he thought while running after the waggon. But queer things were happening inside it.

It was, of course, Milly who had screamed under the sack-bags, being obliged to let off her bitter rage and shame in that way at what Tony was saying, and never daring to show, for very pride and dread o' being laughed at, that she was in hiding. She became more and more restless, and in twisting herself about, what did she see but another woman's foot and white stocking close to her head. It quite frightened her, not knowing that Unity Sallet was in the waggon likewise. But after the fright was over she determined to get to the bottom of all this, and she crept and crept along the bed of the waggon, under the tarpaulin, like a snake, when lo and behold she came face to face with Unity.

'Well, if this isn't disgraceful!' says Milly in a raging whisper to Unity.

''Tis,' says Unity, 'to see you hiding in a young man's waggon like this, and no great character belonging to either of ye!'

'Mind what you are saying!' replied Milly, getting louder. 'I am engaged to be married to him, and haven't I a right to be here? What right have you, I should like to know? What has he been promising you? A pretty lot of nonsense, I expect! But what Tony says to other women is all mere wind, and no concern to me!'

'Don't you be too sure!' says Unity. 'He's going to have Hannah, and not you, nor me either; I could hear that!'

Now at these strange voices sounding from under the cloth Hannah was thunderstruck a'most into a swound; and it was just at this time that the horse moved on. Hannah tugged away wildly, not knowing what she was doing; and as the quarrel rose louder and louder Hannah got so horrified that she let go the reins altogether. The horse went on at his own pace, and coming to the corner where we turn round to drop down the hill to Lower Longpuddle he turned too quick, the off wheels went up the bank, the waggon rose sideways till it was quite on edge upon the near axles, and out rolled the three maidens into the road in a heap. The horse looked round and stood still.

When Tony came up, frightened and breathless, he was relieved enough to see that none of his darlings was hurt, beyond a few scratches from the brambles of the hedge. But he was rather alarmed when he heard how they were going on at one another.

'Don't ye quarrel, my dears – don't ye!' says he, taking off his hat out of respect to 'em. And then he would have kissed them all round, as fair and square as a man could, but they were in too much of a taking to let him, and screeched and sobbed till they was quite spent.

'Now I'll speak out honest, because I ought to,' says Tony, as soon as he could get heard. 'And this is the truth,' says he. 'I've asked Hannah to be mine, and she is willing, and we are going to put up the banns next – '

Tony had not noticed that Hannah's father was coming up behind, nor had he noticed that Hannah's face was beginning to bleed from the scratch of a bramble. Hannah had seen her father, and had run to him, crying worse than ever.

'My daughter is *not* willing, sir!' says Mr Jolliver hot and strong. 'Be you willing, Hannah? I ask ye to have spirit enough to refuse him, if yer virtue is left to 'ee and you run no risk?'

'She's as sound as a bell for me, that I'll swear!' says Tony, flaring up. 'And so's the others, come to that, though you may think it an onusual thing in me!'

'I have spirit, and I do refuse him!' says Hannah, partly because her father was there, and partly, too, in a tantrum because of the discovery, and the scratch that might be left on her face. 'Little did I think when I was so soft with him just now that I was talking to such a false deceiver!'

'What, you won't have me, Hannah?' says Tony, his jaw hanging down like a dead man's.

'Never – I would sooner marry no – nobody at all!' she gasped out, though with her heart in her throat, for she would not have refused Tony if he had asked her quietly, and her father had not been there, and her face had not been scratched by the bramble. And having said that, away she walked upon her father's arm, thinking and hoping he would ask her again.

Tony didn't know what to say next. Milly was sobbing her heart out; but as his father had strongly recommended her he couldn't feel inclined that way. So he turned to Unity.

'Well, will you, Unity dear, be mine?' he says.

'Take her leavings? Not I!' says Unity. 'I'd scorn it!' And away walks Unity Sallet likewise, though she looked back when she'd gone some way, to see if he was following her.

So there at last were left Milly and Tony by themselves, she crying in watery streams, and Tony looking like a tree struck by lightning.

'Well, Milly,' he says at last, going up to her, 'it do seem as if fate had ordained that it should be you and I, or nobody. And what must be must be, I suppose. Hey, Milly?'

'If you like, Tony. You didn't really mean what you said to them?'

'Not a word of it!' declares Tony, bringing down his fist upon his palm.

And then he kissed her, and put the waggon to rights, and they mounted together; and their banns were put up the very next Sunday. I was not able to go to their wedding, but it was a rare party they had, by all account.

Arnold Bennett 1867–1931

Born in the Staffordshire Potteries in 1867, Bennett invented the term 'The Five Towns' to describe the conurbation around Stoke on Trent. Many of his novels and short stories are set in this area.

Bennett was raised in a family of modest means; his father had left school at 12 to become a potter and rose to become a partner in a small pottery firm. When this failed, he worked from home as a pawn broker, before finally becoming a minor solicitor.

The young Arnold did well at school – he passed the examination for the local High School but was not allowed to attend. He left at sixteen to become an unpaid lawyer's clerk. At the age of 21 he left home and moved to London, where he worked for a firm of solicitors. His biographer describes Bennett at this time as a 'modest and highly impressionable observer from the provinces.'

Once in London, Bennett started to write. At the age of 24 he entered a competition in the popular weekly magazine *Tit Bits* and won the first prize of twenty guineas. A period of freelance writing followed, for a variety of magazines. In 1895 the prestigious, *Yellow Book* published his *A Letter Home* and this was very favourably received. Also at this time he abandoned his steady career in law for the far more unpredictable world of journalism, becoming first assitant editor, then editor of *Woman* magazine.

Bennett took all his writing seriously, studying a range of European writers, particularly De Maupassant who was a great favourite of his. He also paid scholarly attention to his newly chosen profession of journalism aimed at women – writing a series of well researched essays on the subject.

From 1895 until he moved to France in 1903, Bennett wrote most of the short stories later to be collected in the anthologies – *Tales of the Five Towns* (1905) and *The Grim Smile of the Five Towns* (1907). *News of the Engagement* is from the second collection and is rooted in the life of the Potteries, with Bursley standing for Burslem and Knype representing Stoke itself. The subject matter of the London based son returning to his middle-class Midland home with important news, has obvious links with Bennett's own domestic experience. But the story's surprise ending, with its powerful consideration of the role and rights of women, owes more perhaps, to his time as editor and magazine journalist.

Bennett's best known novels were to follow quickly – *The Old Wives' Tale* published in 1908 firmly established him as a popular and therefore commercially successful writer. The well known *Clayhanger* series, begun in 1990, was to seal Bennett's reputation as an author of substance. He died of typhoid in 1931 at the age of sixty four.

News of the Engagement

Arnold Bennett

My mother never came to meet me at Bursley station when I arrived in the Five Towns from London; much less did she come as far as Knype station, which is the great traffic centre of the district, the point at which one changes from the express into the local train. She had always other things to do; she was 'preparing' for me. So I had the little journey from Knype to Bursley, and then the walk up Trafalgar Road, amid the familiar high chimneys and the smoke and the clayey mud and the football posters and the Midland accent, all by myself. And there was leisure to consider anew how I should break to my mother the tremendous news I had for her. I had been considering that question ever since getting into the train at Euston, where I had said good-bye to Agnes; but in the atmosphere of the Five Towns it seemed just slightly more difficult; though, of course, it wasn't difficult, really.

You see, I wrote to my mother regularly every week, telling her most of my doings. She knew all my friends by name. I dare say she formed in her mind notions of what sort of people they were. Thus I had frequently mentioned Agnes and her family in my letters. But you can't write even to your mother and say in cold blood: 'I think I am beginning to fall in love with Agnes', 'I think Agnes likes me', 'I am mad on her', 'I feel certain she likes me', 'I shall propose to her on such a day'. You can't do that. At least I couldn't. Hence it had come about that on the 20th of December I had proposed to Agnes and been accepted by Agnes, and my mother had no suspicion that my happiness was so near. And on the 22nd, by a previous and unalterable arrangement, I had come to spend Christmas with my mother.

I was the only son of a widow; I was all that my mother had. And lo! I had gone and engaged myself to a girl she had never seen, and I had kept her in the dark! She would certainly be extremely surprised, and she might be a little bit hurt – just at first. Anyhow, the situation was the least in the world delicate.

I walked up the whitened front steps of my mother's little house, just opposite where the electric cars stop, but before I could put my hand on the bell my little plump mother, in her black silk and her gold brooch and her auburn hair, opened to me, having doubtless watched me down the road from the bay-window, as usual, and she said, as usual, kissing me,

'Well, Philip! How are you?'

And I said,

'Oh! I'm all right, mother. How are you?'

I perceived instantly that she was more excited than my arrival ordinarily made her. There were tears in her smiling eyes, and she was as nervous as a young girl. She did indeed look remarkably young for a woman of forty-five, with twenty-five years of widowhood and a brief but too tempestuous married life behind her.

The thought flashed across my mind: 'By some means or other she has got wind of my engagement. But how?'

But I said nothing. I, too, was naturally rather nervous. Mothers are kittle cattle.

'I'll tell her at supper,' I decided.

And she hovered round me, like a sea-gull round a steamer, as I went upstairs.

There was a ring at the door. She flew, instead of letting the servant go. It was a porter with my bag.

Just as I was coming downstairs again there was another ring at the door. And my mother appeared magically out of the kitchen, but I was beforehand with her, and with a laugh I insisted on opening the front door myself this time. A young woman stood on the step.

'Please, Mrs Dawson wants to know if Mrs Durance can kindly lend her half-a-dozen knives and forks?'

'Eh, with pleasure,' said my mother, behind me. 'Just wait a minute, Lucy. Come inside on the mat.'

I followed my mother into the drawing-room, where she kept her silver in a cabinet.

'That's Mrs Dawson's new servant,' my mother whispered. 'But she needn't think I'm going to lend her my best, because I'm not.'

'I shouldn't, if I were you,' I supported her.

And she went out with some second-best in tissue paper, and beamed on Mrs Dawson's servant with an assumed benevolence.

'There!' she exclaimed. 'And the compliments of the season to your mistress, Lucy.'

After that my mother disappeared into the kitchen to worry an entirely capable servant. And I roamed about, feeling happily excited, examining the drawing-room, in which nothing was changed except the incandescent light and the picture postcards on the mantelpiece. Then I wandered into the dining-room, a small room at the back of the house, and here an immense surprise awaited me.

Supper was set for three!

'Well,' I reflected. 'Here's a nice state of affairs! Supper for three, and she hasn't breathed a word!'

My mother was so clever in social matters, and especially in the planning of delicious surprises, that I believed her capable even of miracles. In some way or other she must have discovered the state of my desires towards Agnes. She had written, or something. She and Agnes had been plotting together by letter to startle me, and perhaps telegraphing. Agnes had fibbed in telling me that she could not possibly come to Bursley for Christmas; she had delightfully fibbed. And my mother had got her concealed somewhere in the house, or was momentarily expecting her. That explained the tears, the nervousness, the rushes to the door.

I crept out of the dining-room, determined not to let my mother know that I had secretly viewed the supper-table. And as I was crossing the lobby to the drawing-room there was a third ring at the door, and a third time my mother rushed out of the kitchen.

'By jove!' I thought. 'Suppose it's Agnes. What a scene!'

And trembling with expectation I opened the door.

It was Mr Nixon.

Now, Mr Nixon was an old friend of the family's, a man of forty-nine or fifty, with a reputation for shrewdness and increasing wealth. He owned a hundred and seventy-five cottages in the town, having bought them gradually in half-dozens, and in rows; he collected the rents himself, and attended to the repairs himself, and was celebrated as a good landlord, and as being almost the only man in Bursley who had made cottage property pay. He lived alone in Commerce Street, and, though not talkative, was usually jolly, with one or two good stories tucked away in the corners of his memory. He was my mother's trustee, and had morally aided her in the troublous times before my father's early death.

'Well, young man,' cried he. 'So you're back in owd Bosley!' It amused him to speak the dialect a little occasionally.

And he brought his burly, powerful form into the lobby.

I greeted him as jovially as I could, and then he shook hands with my mother, neither of them speaking.

'Mr Nixon is come for supper, Philip,' said my mother.

I liked Mr Nixon, but I was not too well pleased by this information, for I wanted to talk confidentially to my mother. I had a task before me with my mother, and here Mr Nixon was plunging into the supper. I could not break it gently to my mother that I was engaged to a strange young woman in the presence of Mr Nixon. Mr Nixon had been in to supper several times during previous visits of mine, but never on the first night.

However, I had to make the best of it. And we sat down and began on the ham, the sausages, the eggs, the crumpets, the toast, the jams, the mince-tarts, the Stilton, and the celery. But we none of us ate very much, despite my little plump mother's protestations.

My suspicion was that perhaps something had gone slightly wrong with my mother's affairs, and that Mr Nixon was taking the first opportunity to explain things to me. But such a possibility did not interest me, for I could easily afford to keep my mother and a wife too. I was still preoccupied in my engagement – and surely there is nothing astonishing in that – and I began to compose the words in which, immediately on the departure of Mr Nixon after supper, I would tackle my mother on the subject.

When we had reached the Stilton and celery, I intimated that I must walk down to the post-office, as I had to dispatch a letter.

'Won't it do tomorrow, my pet?' asked my mother.

'It will not,' I said.

Imagine leaving Agnes two days without news of my safe arrival and without assurances of my love! I had started writing the letter in the train, near Willesden, and I finished it in the drawing-room.

'A lady in the case?', Mr Nixon called out gaily.

'Yes,' I replied with firmness.

I went forth, bought a picture postcard showing St Luke's Square, Bursley, most untruthfully picturesque, and posted the card and the letter to my darling Agnes. I hoped that Mr Nixon would have departed ere my return; he had made no reference at all during supper to my mother's affairs. But he had not departed. I found him solitary in the drawing-room, smoking a very fine cigar.

'Where's the mater?' I demanded.

'She's just gone out of the room,' he said. 'Come and sit down. Have a weed. I want a bit of a chat with you, Philip.'

I obeyed, taking one of the very fine cigars.

'Well, Uncle Nixon,' I encouraged him, wishing to get the chat over because my mind was full of Agnes. I sometimes called him uncle for fun.

'Well, my boy,' he began. 'It's no use me beating about the bush. What do you think of me as a stepfather?'

I was struck, as they say down there, all of a heap.

'What?' I stammered. 'You don't mean to say – you and mother – ?'

He nodded.

'Yes, I do, lad. Yesterday she promised as she'd marry my unworthy self. It's been coming along for some time. But I don't expect she's given you any hint in her letters. In fact, I know she hasn't. It would have been rather difficult, wouldn't it? She couldn't well have written, "My dear Philip, an old friend, Mr Nixon, is falling in love with me and I believe I'm falling in love with him. One of these days he'll be proposing to me." She couldn't have written like that, could she?'

I laughed. I could not help it.

'Shake hands,' I said warmly. 'I'm delighted.'

And soon afterwards my mother sidled in, shyly.

'The lad's delighted, Sarah,' said Mr Nixon shortly.

I said nothing about my own engagement that night. I had never thought of my mother as a woman with a future. I had never realized that she was desirable, and that a man might desire her, and that her lonely existence in that house was not all that she had the right to demand from life. And I was ashamed of my characteristic filial selfish egoism. So I decided that I would not intrude my joy on hers until the next morning. We live and learn.

Elizabeth Gaskell 1810–1865

Elizabeth Gaskell was born in Chelsea in London in 1810. Her father was a Christian minister, a Unitarian, who came to believe that earning money by preaching was wrong and took to earning a living in other ways. Her mother died when she was one year old, and she was brought up by her Aunt Lumb at Knutsford in Cheshire. In 1832 she married a Unitarian minister called William Gaskell and settled in Manchester.

Her home life was busy. She had four daughters and one son, who died of scarlet fever in infancy; she worked with her husband carrying out religious and educational duties. In 1847 her first story was published. From that time until her sudden death in 1865 she wrote novels, short stories and articles for publication. Her first novel *Mary Barton* was a considerable success and from 1848 onwards she was able to supplement the family income with her earnings as a writer contributing to magazines such as *Household Words* and *All the Year Round* run by Charles Dickens.

Elizabeth Gaskell's Unitarian religion was a direct, practical faith which emphasised the importance of tolerance and reason. Her religious and political convictions are reflected in her writing. Her earliest pieces were basically Sunday School stories; in later work she showed a sympathy for problems of Victorian factory workers and for those suffering from poor housing, ill health or poverty. *The Half Brothers,* first published in November 1858, is typical of her strong moral sense and interest in the difficulties faced by ordinary families. The sad, and perhaps rather sentimental, ending to the story is also typical of Elizabeth Gaskell's work, and of much Victorian fiction. Commenting privately on Elizabeth Gaskell's fondness for death-bed scenes and long delirious illnesses brought about by grief, Dickens wrote to his sub-editor: 'I wish to Heaven her people would keep a little firmer on their legs!' But both Dickens and Charlotte Brontë, whose biography Gaskell wrote soon after Charlotte Brontë's death, admired her work and she has had a devoted following of readers from that time to this.

The Half Brothers

Elizabeth Gaskell

My mother was twice married. She never spoke of her first husband, and it is only from other people that I have learnt what little I know about him. I believe she was scarcely seventeen when she was married to him: and he was barely one-and-twenty. He rented a small farm up in Cumberland, somewhere towards the sea-coast; but he was perhaps too young and inexperienced to have the charge of land and cattle: anyhow, his affairs did not prosper, and he fell into ill health, and died of consumption before they had been three years man and wife, leaving my mother a young widow of twenty, with a little child only just able to walk, and the farm on her hands for four years more by the lease, with half the stock on it dead, or sold off one by one to pay the more pressing debts, and with no money to purchase more, or even to buy the provisions needed for the small consumption of every day. There was another child coming, too; and sad and sorry, I believe, she was to think of it. A dreary winter she must have had in her lonesome dwelling, with never another near it for miles around; her sister came to bear her company, and they two planned and plotted how to make every penny they could raise go as far as possible. I can't tell you how it happened that my little sister, whom I never saw, came to sicken and die; but, as if my poor mother's cup was not full enough, only a fortnight before Gregory was born the little girl took ill of scarlet fever, and in a week she lay dead. My mother was, I believe, just stunned with this last blow. My aunt has told me that she did not cry; aunt Fanny would have been thankful if she had; but she sat holding the poor wee lassie's hand, and looking in her pretty, pale, dead face, without so much as shedding a tear. And it was all the same, when they had to take her away to be buried. She just kissed the child, and sat her down in the window-seat to watch the little black train of people (neighbours – my aunt, and one far-off cousin, who were all the friends they could muster) go winding away amongst the snow, which had fallen thinly over the country the night before. When my aunt came back from the funeral, she found my mother in the same place, and as dry-eyed as ever. So she continued until after Gregory was born; and, somehow, his coming seemed to loosen the tears, and she cried day and night, day and night, till my aunt and the other watcher looked at each other in dismay, and would fain* have stopped her if they had but known how. But she bade them let her alone, and not be over-anxious, for every drop she shed eased her brain, which had been in a terrible state before for want of the power to cry. She seemed after that to think of nothing but her new little baby; she hardly appeared to remember either her husband or her little daughter that lay dead in Brigham churchyard – at least so aunt Fanny said; but she was a great talker, and my mother was very silent by nature, and I think aunt Fanny may have been mistaken in believing that my mother never thought of her husband and child just because she never spoke about them. Aunt Fanny was older than my mother, and had a way of treating her like a child; but, for all that, she was a kind, warm-hearted creature, who thought more of her sister's welfare than she did of her own; and it was on her bit of money that they principally lived, and on what the two could earn by working for the great Glasgow sewing-merchants. But by-and-by my mother's eyesight began to fail. It was not that she was exactly blind, for she could see well enough to guide herself about the house, and to do a good deal of domestic work; but she could no longer do fine sewing and earn money. It must have been with the heavy crying she had had in her day, for she was but a young creature at this time, and as pretty a young woman, I have heard people say, as any on the country side. She took it sadly to heart that she could no longer gain anything towards the keep of herself and her child. My aunt Fanny would fain have

* gladly

persuaded her that she had enough to do in managing their cottage and minding Gregory; but my mother knew that they were pinched, and that aunt Fanny herself had not as much to eat, even of the commonest kind of food, as she could have done with; and as for Gregory, he was not a strong lad, and needed, not more food – for he always had enough, whoever went short – but better nourishment, and more flesh-meat. One day – it was aunt Fanny who told me all this about my poor mother, long after her death – as the sisters were sitting together, aunt Fanny working, and my mother hushing Gregory to sleep, William Preston, who was afterwards my father, came in. He was reckoned an old bachelor; I suppose he was long past forty, and he was one of the wealthiest farmers thereabouts, and had known my grandfather well, and my mother and my aunt in their more prosperous days. He sat down, and began to twirl his hat by way of being agreeable; my aunt Fanny talked, and he listened and looked at my mother. But he said very little, either on that visit, or on many another that he paid before he spoke out what had been the real purpose of his calling so often all along, and from the very first time he came to their house. One Sunday, however, my aunt Fanny stayed away from church, and took care of the child, and my mother went alone. When she came back, she ran straight upstairs, without going into the kitchen to look at Gregory or speak any word to her sister, and aunt Fanny heard her cry as if her heart was breaking; so she went up and scolded her right well through the bolted door, till at last she got her to open it. And then she threw herself on my aunt's neck, and told her that William Preston had asked her to marry him, and had promised to take good charge of her boy, and to let him want for nothing, neither in the way of keep nor of education, and that she had consented. Aunt Fanny was a good deal shocked at this; for, as I have said, she had often thought that my mother had forgotten her first husband very quickly, and now here was proof positive of it, if she could so soon think of marrying again. Besides, as aunt Fanny used to say, she herself would have been a far more suitable match for a man of William Preston's age than Helen, who, though she was a widow, had not seen her four-and-twentieth summer. However, as aunt Fanny said, they had not asked her advice; and there was much to be said on the other side of the question. Helen's eyesight would never be good for much again, and as William Preston's wife she would never need to do anything, if she chose to sit with her hands before her; and a boy was a great charge to a widowed mother; and now there would be a decent, steady man to see after him. So, by-and-by, aunt Fanny seemed to take a brighter view of the marriage than did my mother herself, who hardly ever looked up, and never smiled after the day when she promised William Preston to be his wife. But much as she had loved Gregory before, she seemed to love him more now. She was continually talking to him when they were alone, though he was far too young to understand her moaning words, or give her any comfort, except by his caresses.

At last William Preston and she were wed; and she went to be mistress of a well-stocked house, not above half an hour's walk from where aunt Fanny lived. I believe she did all that she could to please my father; and a more dutiful wife, I have heard him himself say, could never have been. But she did not love him, and he soon found it out. She loved Gregory, and she did not love him. Perhaps, love would have come in time, if he had been patient enough to wait; but it just turned him sour to see how her eye brightened and her colour came at the sight of that little child, while for him who had given her so much, she had only gentle words as cold as ice. He got to taunt her with the difference in her manner, as if that would bring love: and he took a positive dislike to Gregory, – he was so jealous of the ready love that always gushed out like a spring of fresh water when he came near. He wanted her to love him more, and perhaps that was all well and good; but he wanted her to love her child less, and that was an evil wish. One day, he gave way to his temper, and cursed and swore at Gregory, who had got into some mischief, as children will; my mother made some excuse for him; my father said it was hard enough to have to keep another man's child, without having it perpetually held up in its naughtiness by his wife, who ought to be always in the same mind that he was; and so from little they got to more;

and the end of it was, that my mother took to her bed before her time, and I was born that very day. My father was glad, and proud, and sorry, all in a breath; glad and proud that a son was born to him; and sorry for his poor wife's state, and to think how his angry words had brought it on. But he was a man who liked better to be angry than sorry, so he soon found out that it was all Gregory's fault, and owed him an additional grudge for having hastened my birth. He had another grudge against him before long. My mother began to sink the day after I was born. My father sent to Carlisle for doctors, and would have coined his heart's blood into gold to save her, if that could have been; but it could not. My aunt Fanny used to say sometimes, that she thought that Helen did not wish to live, and so just let herself die away without trying to take hold on life; but when I questioned her, she owned that my mother did all the doctors bade her do, with the same sort of uncomplaining patience with which she had acted through life. One of her last requests was to have Gregory laid in her bed by my side, and then she made him take hold of my little hand. Her husband came in while she was looking at us so, and when he bent tenderly over her to ask her how she felt now, and seemed to gaze on us two little half-brothers, with a grave sort of kindliness, she looked up in his face and smiled, almost her first smile at him; and such a sweet smile! as more besides aunt Fanny have said. In an hour she was dead. Aunt Fanny came to live with us. It was the best thing that could be done. My father would have been glad to return to his old mode of bachelor life, but what could he do with two little children? He needed a woman to take care of him, and who so fitting as his wife's elder sister? So she had the charge of me from my birth; and for a time I was weakly, as was but natural, and she was always beside me, night and day watching over me, and my father nearly as anxious as she. For his land had come down from father to son for more than three hundred years, and he would have cared for me merely as his flesh and blood that was to inherit the land after him. But he needed something to love, for all that, to most people, he was a stern, hard man, and he took to me as, I fancy, he had taken to no human being before – as he might have taken to my mother, if she had had no former life for him to be jealous of. I loved him back again right heartily. I loved all around me, I believe, for everybody was kind to me. After a time, I overcame my original weakliness of constitution, and was just a bonny, strong-looking lad whom every passer-by noticed, when my father took me with him to the nearest town.

At home I was the darling of my aunt, the tenderly-beloved of my father, the pet and plaything of the old domestic, the 'young master' of the farm-labourers, before whom I played many a lordly antic, assuming a sort of authority which sat oddly enough, I doubt not, on such a baby as I was.

Gregory was three years older than I. Aunt Fanny was always kind to him in deed and in action, but she did not often think about him, she had fallen so completely into the habit of being engrossed by me, from the fact of my having come into her charge as a delicate baby. My father never got over his grudging dislike to his stepson, who had so innocently wrestled with him for the possession of my mother's heart. I mistrust me, too, that my father always considered him as the cause of my mother's death and my early delicacy; and utterly unreasonable as this may seem, I believe my father rather cherished his feeling of alienation to my brother as a duty, than strove to repress it. Yet not for the world would my father have grudged him anything that money could purchase. That was, as it were, in the bond when he had wedded my mother. Gregory was lumpish and loutish, awkward and ungainly, marring whatever he meddled in, and many a hard word and sharp scolding did he get from the people about the farm, who hardly waited till my father's back was turned before they rated the stepson. I am ashamed – my heart is sore to think how I fell into the fashion of the family, and slighted my poor orphan step-brother. I don't think I ever scouted him, or was wilfully ill-natured to him; but the habit of being considered in all things, and being treated as something uncommon and superior, made me insolent in my prosperity, and I exacted more than Gregory was always willing to grant, and then, irritated, I sometimes repeated the disparaging words I had heard others use with regard to him, without fully understanding their meaning. Whether he did or not I cannot tell. I am afraid he did. He used to turn silent and quiet – sullen and sulky, my father thought it; stupid, aunt Fanny used to call it. But every one said he was stupid and dull, and this stupidity and dullness grew upon him. He would sit without speaking a word, sometimes, for hours; then my father would bid him rise and do some piece of work, maybe, about the farm. And he would take three of four tellings before he would go. When we were sent to school, it was all the same. He could never be made to remember his lessons; the schoolmaster grew weary of scolding and flogging, and at last advised my father just to take him away, and set him to some farm-work that might not be above his comprehension. I think he was more gloomy and stupid than ever after this, yet he was not a cross lad; he was patient and good-natured, and would try to do a kind turn for any one, even if they had been scolding or cuffing him not a minute before. But very often his attempts at kindness ended in some mischief to the very people he was trying to serve, owing to his awkward, ungainly ways. I suppose I was a clever lad; at any rate, I always got plenty of praise; and was, as we called it, the cock of the school. The schoolmaster said I could learn anything I chose, but my father, who had no great learning himself, saw little use in much for me, and took me away betimes,* and kept me with him about the farm. Gregory was made into a kind of shepherd, receiving his training under old Adam, who was nearly past his work. I think old Adam was almost the first person who had a good opinion of Gregory. He stood to it that my brother had good parts, though he did not rightly know how to bring them out; and, for knowing the bearings of the Fells, he said he had never seen a lad like him. My father would try to bring Adam round to speak of Gregory's faults and shortcomings; but, instead of that, he would praise him twice as much as soon as he found out what was my father's object.

One winter-time, when I was about sixteen, and Gregory nineteen, I was sent by my father on an errand to a place

* early

about seven miles distant by the road, but only about four by the Fells. He bade me return by the road, whichever way I took in going, for the evenings closed in early, and were often thick and misty; besides which, old Adam, now paralytic and bedridden, foretold a downfall of snow before long. I soon got to my journey's end, and soon had done my business; earlier by an hour, I thought, than my father had expected, so I took the decision of the way by which I would return into my own hands, and set off back again over the Fells, just as the first shades of evening began to fall. It looked dark and gloomy enough; but everything was so still that I thought I should have plenty of time to get home before the snow came down. Off I set at a pretty quick pace. But night came on quicker. The right path was clear enough in the daytime, although at several points two or three exactly similar diverged from the same place; but when there was a good light, the traveller was guided by the sight of distant objects, – a piece of rock, – a fall in the ground – which were quite invisible to me now. I plucked up a brave heart, however, and took what seemed to me the right road. It was wrong, however, and led me whither I knew not, but to some wild boggy moor where the solitude seemed painful, intense, as if never footfall of man had come thither to break the silence. I tried to shout, – with the dimmest possible hope of being heard – rather to reassure myself by the sound of my own voice; but my voice came husky and short, and yet it dismayed me; it seemed so weird and strange in that noiseless expanse of black darkness. Suddenly the air was filled thick with dusky flakes, my face and hands were wet with snow. It cut me off from the slightest knowledge of where I was, for I lost every idea of the direction from which I had come, so that I could not even retrace my steps; it hemmed me in, thicker, thicker, with a darkness that might be felt. The boggy soil on which I stood quaked under me if I remained long in one place, and yet I dared not move far. All my youthful hardiness seemed to leave me at once. I was on the point of crying, and only very shame seemed to keep it down. To save myself from shedding tears, I shouted – terrible, wild shouts for bare life they were. I turned sick as I paused to listen; no answering sound came but the unfeeling echoes. Only the noiseless, pitiless snow kept falling thicker, thicker – faster, faster! I was growing numb and sleepy. I tried to move about, but I dared not go far, for fear of the precipices which, I knew, abounded in certain places on the Fells. Now and then, I stood still and shouted again; but my voice was getting choked with tears, as I thought of the desolate, helpless death I was to die, and how little they at home, sitting round the warm, red, bright fire, wotted* what was become of me, – and how my poor father would grieve for me – it would surely kill him – it would break his heart, poor old man! Aunt Fanny too – was this to be the end of all her cares for me? I began to review my life in a strange kind of vivid dream, in which the various scenes of my few boyish years passed before me like visions. In a pang of agony, caused by such remembrance of my short life, I gathered up my strength and called out once more, a long, despairing, wailing cry, to which I had no hope of obtaining any answer, save from the echoes around, dulled as the sound might be by the thickened air. To my surprise, I heard a cry – almost as long, as wild as mine – so wild that it seemed unearthly, and I almost thought it must be the voice of some of the mocking spirits of the Fells, about whom I had heard so many tales. My heart suddenly began to beat fast and loud. I could not reply for a minute or two. I nearly fancied I had lost the power of utterance. Just at this moment a dog barked. Was it Lassie's bark – my brother's collie? – an ugly enough brute, with a white, ill-looking face, that my father always kicked whenever he saw it, partly for its own demerits, partly because it belonged to my brother. On such occasions, Gregory would whistle Lassie away, and go off and sit with her in some outhouse. My father had once or twice been ashamed of himself, when the poor collie had yowled out with the suddenness of the pain, and had relieved himself of his self-reproach by blaming my brother, who, he said, had no notion of training a dog, and was enough to ruin any collie in Christendom with his stupid way of allowing them to lie by the kitchen fire. To

* were aware of

all which Gregory would answer nothing, nor even seem to hear, but go on looking absent and moody.

Yes! there again! It was Lassie's bark! Now or never! I lifted up my voice and shouted 'Lassie! Lassie! For God's sake, Lassie!' Another moment, and the great white-faced Lassie was curving and gambolling with delight round my feet and legs, looking, however, up in my face with her intelligent, apprehensive eyes, as if fearing lest I might greet her with a blow, as I had done oftentimes before. But I cried with gladness, as I stooped down and patted her. My mind was sharing in my body's weakness, and I could not reason, but I knew that help was at hand. A grey figure came more and more distinctly out of the thick, close-pressing darkness. It was Gregory wrapped in his maud.*

'Oh, Gregory!' said I, and I fell upon his neck, unable to speak another word. He never spoke much, and made me no answer for some little time. Then he told me we must move, we must walk for the dear life – we must find our road home, if possible; but we must move or we should be frozen to death.

'Don't you know the way home?' asked I.

'I thought I did when I set out, but I am doubtful now. The snow blinds me, and I am feared that in moving about just now, I have lost the right gait homewards.'

He had his shepherd's staff with him, and by dint of plunging it before us at every step we took – clinging close to each other, we went on safely enough, as far as not falling down any of the steep rocks, but it was slow, dreary work. My brother, I saw, was more guided by Lassie and the way she took than anything else, trusting to her instinct. It was too dark to see far before us; but he called her back continually, and noted from what quarter she returned, and shaped our slow steps accordingly. But the tedious motion scarcely kept my very blood from freezing. Every bone, every fibre in my body seemed first to ache, and then to swell, and then to turn numb with the intense cold. My brother bore it better than I, from having been more out upon the hills. He did not speak, except to call

* woollen shawl

Lassie. I strove to be brave, and not complain; but now I felt the deadly fatal sleep stealing over me.

'I can go no farther,' I said, in a drowsy tone. I remember I suddenly became dogged and resolved. Sleep I would, were it only for five minutes. If death were to be the consequence, sleep I would. Gregory stood still. I suppose, he recognized the peculiar phase of suffering to which I had been brought by the cold.

'It is of no use,' said he, as if to himself. 'We are no nearer home than we were when we started, as far as I can tell. Our only chance is in Lassie. Here! roll thee in my maud, lad, and lay thee down on this sheltered side of this bit of rock. Creep close under it, lad, and I'll lie by thee, and strive to keep the warmth in us. Stay! hast gotten aught about thee they'll know at home?'

I felt him unkind thus to keep me from slumber, but on his repeating the question, I pulled out my pocket-handkerchief, of some showy pattern, which aunt Fanny had hemmed for me – Gregory took it, and tied it round Lassie's neck.

'Hie thee, Lassie, hie thee home!' And the white-faced, ill-favoured brute was off like a shot in the darkness. Now I might lie down – now I might sleep. In my drowsy stupor I felt that I was being tenderly covered up by my brother; but what with I neither knew nor cared – I was too dull, too selfish, too numb to think and reason, or I might have known that in that bleak bare place there was naught to wrap me in, save what was taken off another. I was glad enough when he ceased his cares and lay down by me. I took his hand.

'Thou canst not remember, lad, how we lay together thus by our dying mother. She put thy small, wee hand in mine – I reckon she sees us now; and belike we shall soon be with her. Anyhow, God's will be done.'

'Dear Gregory,' I muttered, and crept nearer to him for warmth. He was talking still, and again about our mother, when I fell asleep. In an instant – or so it seemed – there were many voices about me – many faces hovering round me – the sweet luxury of warmth was stealing into every part of me. I was in my own little bed at home. I am thankful to say, my first word was 'Gregory?'

A look passed from one to another – my father's stern old face strove in vain to keep its sternness; his mouth quivered, his eyes filled slowly with unwonted tears.

'I would have given him half my land – I would have blessed him as my son, – oh God! I would have knelt at his feet, and asked him to forgive my hardness of heart.'

I heard no more. A whirl came through my brain, catching me back to death.

I came slowly to my consciousness, weeks afterwards. My father's hair was white when I recovered, and his hands shook as he looked into my face.

We spoke no more of Gregory. We could not speak of him; but he was strangely in our thoughts. Lassie came and went with never a word of blame; nay, my father would try to stroke her, but she shrank away; and he, as if reproved by the poor dumb beast, would sigh, and be silent and abstracted for a time.

Aunt Fanny – always a talker – told me all. How, on that fatal night, my father, irritated by my prolonged absence, and probably more anxious than he cared to show, had been fierce and imperious, even beyond his wont, to Gregory: had upbraided him with his father's poverty, his own stupidity which made his services good for nothing – for so, in spite of the old shepherd, my father always chose to consider them. At last, Gregory had risen up, and whistled Lassie out with him – poor Lassie, crouching underneath his chair for fear of a kick or a blow. Some time before, there had been some talk between my father and my aunt respecting my return; and when Aunt Fanny told me all this, she said she fancied that Gregory might have noticed the coming storm, and gone out silently to meet me. Three hours afterwards, when all were running about in wild alarm, not knowing whither to go in search of me – not even missing Gregory, or heeding his absence, poor fellow – poor, poor fellow! – Lassie came home, with my handkerchief tied round her neck. They knew and understood, and the whole strength of the farm was turned out to follow her, with wraps, and blankets, and brandy, and everything that could be thought of. I lay in chilly sleep, but still alive, beneath the rock that Lassie guided them to. I was covered over with my brother's plaid, and his thick shepherd's coat was carefully wrapped round my feet. He was in his shirt-sleeves – his arm thrown over me – a quiet smile (he had hardly ever smiled in life) upon his still, cold face.

My father's last words were, 'God forgive me my hardness of heart towards the fatherless child!'

And what marked the depth of his feeling of repentance, perhaps more than all, considering the passionate love he bore my mother, was this: we found a paper of directions after his death, in which he desired that he might lie at the foot of the grave, in which, by his desire, poor Gregory had been laid with our mother.

Guy de Maupassant 1850–1893

Many writers have been inspired by the example of Guy de Maupassant's stories. Although he was writing for only a relatively short time – eleven years of productive work – he produced over 300 short stories, 200 articles and six novels as well as plays and travel writing. He is admired for his spare and accurate style, as well as for the shape he gave to his stories, with their ironic twists.

Maupassant, full name Henri-René-Albert Guy de Maupassant was born in 1850 in Normandy, France. His father, Gustave, was from a minor aristocratic family and had his own private income; his mother Laure de Potterin was a well-read and cultured woman. Maupassant was sent to a Catholic boarding school which he hated. He reacted fiercely against the strict rules of school life and was finally expelled for writing obscene verses. Maupassant continued his studies at Rouen and Paris, but the outbreak of war and the consequent collapse of his family's fortune forced him to become a poorly paid civil servant. He sought relief from the boredom of life by rowing on the river and chasing young women. It was at this time that he probably caught the venereal disease syphilis which was to cause his later madness and eventual death, at the age of 43.

Encouraged by Gustave Flaubert, a well-known author and childhood friend of his mother, Maupassant took up writing and developed a simple, exact style. His writing soon gained popularity and was published in many newspapers and magazines. He joined the circle of naturalistic writers around Emile Zola; these writers wanted to document the life and suffering of ordinary working people in an accurate, detached way.

The story *Country Living* (1883) deals with the extremes of wealth and poverty which Maupassant saw around him. He describes the dilemma faced by a poor peasant family when they are asked to sell their child to an aristocratic, childless couple. In a surprising and uncomfortable ending readers are forced to confront this difficult moral choice.

Country Living

Guy de Maupassant

The two cottages stood side by side at the foot of a hill not far from a small spa town. The two peasant farmers who lived in them worked very hard cultivating the poor soil to rear all the children they had. Each couple had four, and outside each house the whole gang of them played and shrieked from morning till night. The two oldest were six and the two youngest about fifteen months. Weddings and then births had occurred at more or less the same times in both houses.

The two mothers were none too sure which of the heaving brood were theirs and which were not, and both farmers were quite incapable of telling them apart. The eight names went round and round in their heads and they were forever getting them mixed up. And when one of them was wanted, the men often shouted three names before getting the right one.

The first of these houses, as you come along the road from the spa, which was Rolleport, was occupied by the Tuvaches who had three girls and a boy. The other was home to the Vallins, who had one girl and three boys.

They all lived on a meagre diet of soup, potatoes, and fresh air. At seven in the morning, at noon, and again at six in the evening, the women called their brood in to feed them, rather as a farmer's boy might gather in the geese. The children were seated in order of age at the wooden kitchen table which shone with fifty years of wear. The mouth of the last in line scarcely came up to the top of the table. In front of them was set a bowl containing bread soaked in the water the potatoes had been boiled in, half a cabbage, and three onions: and they all ate until they were full. The mother pushed food into the youngest herself. A small piece of meat in a stew on Sundays was a treat for one and all, and on that day the father usually lingered over his dinner saying: 'I could get used to having that every day of the week.'

One August afternoon, a horse and trap drew up unexpectedly outside the two cottages, and the young woman who had been driving it herself said to the man sitting next to her: 'Oh Henri, do look at those children. Aren't they pretty, rolling around in the dirt like that!'

The man did not answer, for he was used to these sudden enthusiasms which he felt as a physical hurt and took more or less as a personal reproach.

The young woman went on: 'I must kiss them! Oh, how I'd love to have one of them – that one, the tiny one.' And jumping down from the trap, she ran over to the children, picked up one of the two smallest – the Tuvaches' youngest boy – and lifting him in her arms, planted eager kisses on his dirty cheeks, on his curly, blond, mud-daubed hair, and on his little fists which he waved in his efforts to free himself from attentions which he plainly did not like.

Then she got back into the trap and drove off at a smart trot. But she came back the following week, sat herself down on the ground with them, took the little boy in her arms, stuffed him full of cake and handed sweets to all the others. And she played with them as though she were a little girl herself, while her husband waited patiently in their dainty trap.

She came back again, got to know the parents, and began putting in an appearance daily, her pockets bulging with sweeties and pennies.

Her name was Madame Henri d'Hubières.

When she arrived one morning, her husband got down out of the trap with her. Without stopping to talk to the children, who all knew her well by this time, she walked straight up to one of the farmers' cottages.

The farmer and his wife were busy chopping enough firewood to cook the dinner. They straightened up in surprise, brought out chairs, and then waited. Only then did the young woman begin speaking in a broken, trembling voice.

'You dear people, I have come to see you because . . .

because I would very much like . . . I would very much like to . . . to take your little boy away with me.'

Taken completely by surprise and not knowing what to think, the farmer and his wife did not answer.

She paused for breath, then went on: 'We have no children. My husband and I are alone . . . We'd give him a home . . . Would you be willing?'

The mother began to have an inkling of what was going on. She asked: 'You be wanting to take our Charlot away with you? Couldn't have that. No indeed.'

At this point, Monsieur d'Hubières intervened: 'My wife has not made herself clear. We would like to adopt him, but he'd be able to come back and see you. If he turns out well, and everything suggests that he will, one day he will inherit everything we own. If we do by some chance have children, he would share equally with them. But if he does not make the most of his opportunities, we will give him the sum of twenty thousand francs when he comes of age, this sum to be deposited as of now in his name with a lawyer. And because we have also been thinking of you, you will receive a hundred francs a month for as long as you live. Do you understand?'

The farmer's wife rose to her feet like a fury: 'You want us to sell you our Charlot? No. Never! It's a thing nobody's got no right asking a mother to do. I won't have it! It'd be sinful and wicked!'

Her husband, looking grave and thoughtful, said nothing. But he indicated his approval of what his wife said by nodding his head all the time she spoke.

It was all too much for Madame d'Hubières who burst into tears and, turning to her husband, stammered in the tear-choked voice of a little girl who always gets her way: 'They don't want to, Henri, they don't want to!'

They made one last attempt: 'Listen. Think about your son's future, about his happiness, about . . .'

Losing patience, the wife interrupted: 'We've heard you out, we've understood, and we've made up our minds . . . Now just go and don't you ever let me see you round this way again. Never heard the like! The very idea! Wanting to take away a baby just like that!'

As she was leaving, Madame d'Hubières recalled that

there were two little boys and asked, through her tears, and with the persistence of a headstrong, spoilt woman who is not prepared to wait: 'The other little boy isn't yours, is he?'

Monsieur Tuvache answered: 'No. He's next door's. You can go and see them if you like.' And he went back into his house where his wife could be heard complaining indignantly.

The Vallins were sitting round their table, with a plate between them, slowly eating slices of bread thinly spread with rancid butter.

Monsieur d'Hubières restated his proposal to them, but this time he was more subtle, shrewder, and he put honey in his voice.

The man and his wife shook their heads to indicate their unwillingness. But when they learned that they would get a hundred francs a month, they looked at each other, exchanged enquiring glances, and seemed to hesitate.

Torn and uncertain, they did not say anything for some time. In the end, the wife asked her husband: 'Well, what have you got to say?'

He replied sententiously: 'What I say is that it's not to be sneezed at.'

Madame d'Hubières, trembling with anguish, then spoke to them about the future their little boy would have, how happy he would be and how much money he would be able to give them later on.

'This business of the twelve hundred francs,' the man asked, 'it'd be all properly settled by a lawyer?'

'Absolutely,' Monsieur d'Hubières replied. 'It could be all arranged tomorrow.'

The wife, who had been thinking, went on:

'A hundred francs a month, well, it don't compensate us nowhere near for not having our boy around. Give him a couple of years and he'll be old enough to be set to work. We'd need a hundred and twenty.'

Madame d'Hubières was so impatient to finalize matters that she agreed immediately. And since she was anxious to take the child away with her at once, she gave them an extra hundred francs as a present while her husband was drawing up a written agreement. The mayor and a neighbour were hurriedly summoned and willingly witnessed the document.

The young woman, radiant, took the screaming child away as others might bear off a coveted bargain from a shop.

The Tuvaches stood on their doorstep and watched him go, saying nothing, grim-faced, and perhaps regretting that they had said no.

That was the last that was heard of little Jean Vallin. Each month his parents collected their one hundred and twenty francs from the lawyer. They quarrelled with their neighbours, because Madame Tuvache said the most awful things about them and went around other people's houses saying that anyone who sells a child for money must be unnatural, that it was a horrible, disgusting, dirty business. And sometimes she would pick up her little Charlot for all to see and say loudly, as though he could understand: 'I din't sell you, my precious, I din't! I don't go round selling my children. I haven't got a lot of money, but I don't go round selling my children!'

It was the same each day for years and years. Each day coarse jeers were bellowed on one doorstep so that they were heard in the house next door. In the end Madame Tuvache came to believe that she was better than anybody else for miles around because she had refused to sell her little Charlot. And when people talked about her, they said: ''Twas a tempting offer, right enough. But she wasn't interested. She done what a good mother oughter.'

She was held up as a model. Little Charlot, who was now almost 18 and had been brought up having this idea constantly repeated to him, also thought he was a cut above his friends because he had not been sold.

The Vallins pottered along quite comfortably on their pension. Which explains why the fury of the Tuvaches, who remained poor, was so implacable.

Their oldest boy went off to do his military service. The second died and Charlot was left alone to work alongside his old father to support his mother and his two younger sisters.

He was getting on for 21 when, one morning, a gleaming carriage pulled up outside the two cottages. A young gentleman, wearing a gold watch-chain, got out and helped down an old lady with white hair. The old lady said to him: 'It's there, dear. The second house.'

He walked straight into the Vallins' hovel as though it were his own.

Old Madame Vallin was washing her aprons. Her husband, now infirm, was dozing by the fire. Both looked up and the young man said:

'Good morning, mother. Good morning, father.'

They both stood up in dismay. Madame Vallin was in such a state that she dropped her soap into the water. She stammered: 'Is that you, son? Is it really you?'

He took her in his arms and kissed her, repeating: 'Hello, mother.' Meanwhile the old man, shaking all over, kept saying in the calm tone of voice which never deserted him: 'Here you are back again, Jean,' as though he had seen him only the month before.

When they had got over the shock the parents said they wanted to take their boy out and show him off everywhere. They took him to see the mayor, the deputy mayor, the village priest, and the schoolmaster.

Charlot watched them go from the doorstep of the cottage next door.

That night, at supper, he said to his parents: 'You can't have been right in the head letting the Vallin kid get took away.'

His mother replied stubbornly: 'I'd never have let a child of ours get took.'

His father said nothing.

The son went on: 'I really missed the boat the day I got made a sacrifice of.'

At this, old Tuvache said angrily: 'You're not blaming us for keeping you?'

The young man replied cruelly: 'O' course I blame you. I blame you for being so soft in the head. Parents like you is the reason why children get held back. It'd serve you right if I upped sticks and off.'

The old woman cried into her dinner. She gave little moans as she swallowed each mouthful of soup, half of which she spilled: 'You kill yourself to bring up your kids and what thanks do you get?'

Then the lad said roughly: 'I'd as soon have never been born than be as I am. When I saw him from next door earlier on, it come right home to me. I said to meself: that's what I could have been like now!' He stood up. 'Listen, I think it'd be best if I didn't stay around the place, because I'd only be throwing it in your faces morning noon and night. I'd just make your lives a misery. I'll never forgive you. Never.'

The two old people sat in silence, utterly crushed and in tears. He continued: 'I couldn't stand the thought of that. I'd rather go off and make a fresh start somewhere else.'

He opened the door. Through it came the sound of voices. The Vallins were celebrating with their boy who had come back.

Charlot stamped his feet in rage and, turning to his parents, screamed: 'Know what you are? Stupid, bog-trotting yokels!'

And he vanished into the night.

Richard Harding Davis 1864–1916

Richard Harding Davis was born in 1864 in Philadelphia, USA. His mother, Rebecca Harding Davis, was a successful author who wrote stories about the realities of urban industrial life. Brought up amongst literary people, he decided after college to make a career as a writer and found a job as a journalist on a Philadelphia daily newspaper.

Richard Harding Davis enjoyed a highly successful career as newspaper correspondent. He became the leading reporter of his day and was commissioned to write articles which involved him travelling around the world. As a war correspondent at a time of widespread unrest, he reported on the Cuban war, two Balkan wars, the Russo-Japanese war, various South American and Central American disturbances, the Boer war, the early phases of the First World War . . . 'No one,' said Charles Dana Gibson, the illustrator of his stories, 'ever saw more wars in so many different places.' His news stories were vividly and dramatically written and very popular; by the age of 26 he was the managing editor of *Harper's Weekly*, an important magazine.

Richard Harding Davis was known as a man-about-town. He dressed in stylish clothes and enjoyed visiting the various restaurants, clubs and entertainments on offer in the city. He promoted his reputation as a gentleman – whilst in Paris, for example, he was in a theatre where an actress was being hissed at by a rejected lover and his friends. Davis leapt to his feet and demanded that all American and English men join him in silencing the hissers 'to teach them a lesson in Anglo-Saxon fair play.' His image was not dissimilar to that of his hero, Courtland Van Bibber, the rich young clubman that we meet in the story in this collection.

Richard Harding Davis was a prolific writer; in a relatively short life he wrote several novels, 25 plays and over 80 short stories, as well as his journalism. His fiction was often swashbuckling and dramatic, sometimes romantic. In its day it was very popular, although it has been less so since his death in 1916. *Van Bibber and*

Others, the collection from which the following story is taken, was especially successful when it first appeared in 1892: by the second day after publication, 4,000 copies had already been sold.

Van Bibber's Burglar

Richard Harding Davis

There had been a dance up-town, but as Van Bibber could not find Her there, he accepted young Travers's suggestion to go over to Jersey City and see a 'go'* between 'Dutchy' Mack and a coloured person professionally known as the Black Diamond. They covered up all signs of their evening dress with their great-coats, and filled their pockets with cigars for the smoke which surrounds a 'go' is trying to sensitive nostrils, and they also fastened their watches to both key-chains. Alf Alpin, who was acting as master of ceremonies, was greatly pleased and flattered at their coming, and boisterously insisted on their sitting on the platform. The fact was generally circulated among the spectators that the 'two gents in high hats' had come in a carriage, and this and their patent-leather boots made them objects of keen interest. It was even whispered that they were the 'parties' who were putting up the money to back the Black Diamond against the 'Hester Street Jackson.' This in itself entitled them to respect. Van Bibber was asked to hold the watch, but he wisely declined the honour, which was given to Andy Spielman, the sporting reporter of the *Track and Ring*, whose watch-case was covered with diamonds, and was just the sort of a watch a timekeeper should hold.

It was two o'clock before 'Dutchy' Mack's backer threw the sponge into the air, and three before they reached the city. They had another reporter in the cab with them besides the gentleman who had bravely held the watch in the face of several offers to 'do for' him; and as Van Bibber was ravenously hungry, and as he doubted that he could

* boxing match

get anything at that hour at the club, they accepted Spielman's invitation and went for a porterhouse steak and onions at the Owl's Nest, Gus McGowan's all-night restaurant on Third Avenue.

It was a very dingy, dirty place, but it was as warm as the engine-room of a steamboat, and the steak was perfectly done and tender. It was too late to go to bed, so they sat around the table, with their chairs tipped back and their knees against its edge. The two club men had thrown off their great-coats, and their wide shirt fronts and silk facings shone grandly in the smoky light of the oil lamps and the red glow from the grill in the corner. They talked about the life the reporters led, and the Philistines asked foolish questions, which the gentlemen of the press answered without showing them how foolish they were.

'And I suppose you have all sorts of curious adventures,' said Van Bibber, tentatively.

'Well, no, not what I would call adventures,' said one of the reporters. 'I have never seen anything that could not be explained or attributed directly to some known cause, such as crime or poverty or drink. You may think at first that you have stumbled on something strange and romantic, but it comes to nothing. You would suppose that in a great city like this one would come across something that could not be explained away – something mysterious or out of the common, like Stevenson's Suicide Club. But I have not found it so. Dickens once told James Payn that the most curious thing he ever saw in his rambles around London was a ragged man who stood crouching under the window of a great house where the owner was giving a ball. While the man hid beneath a window on the ground floor, a woman wonderfully dressed and very beautiful, raised the sash from the inside and dropped her bouquet down into the man's hand, and he nodded and stuck it under his coat and ran off with it.

'I call that, now, a really curious thing to see. But I have never come across anything like it, and I have been in every part of this big city, and at every hour of the night and morning, and I am not lacking in imagination either, but no captured maidens have ever beckoned to me from barred windows nor 'white hands waved from a passing hansom.' Balzac and De Musset and Stevenson suggest that they have had such adventures, but they never come to me. It is all commonplace and vulgar, and always ends in a police court or with a 'found drowned' in the North River.'

McGowan, who had fallen into a doze behind the bar, woke suddenly and shivered and rubbed his shirt-sleeves briskly. A woman knocked at the side door and begged for a drink 'for the love of heaven,' and the man who tended the grill told her to be off. They could hear her feeling her way against the wall and cursing as she staggered out of the alley. Three men came in with a hack driver and wanted everybody to drink with them, and became insolent when the gentlemen declined, and were in consequence hustled out one at a time by McGowan, who went to sleep again immediately, with his head resting among the cigar-boxes and pyramids of glasses at the back of the bar, and snored.

'You see,' said the reporter, 'it is all like this. Night in a great city is not picturesque and it is not theatrical. It is sodden, sometimes brutal, exciting enough until you get used to it, but it runs in a groove. It is dramatic, but the plot is old and the motives and characters always the same.'

The rumble of heavy market wagons and the rattle of milk carts told them that it was morning, and as they opened the door the cold fresh air swept into the place and made them wrap their collars around their throats and stamp their feet. The morning wind swept down the cross-street from the East River and the lights of the street lamps and of the saloon looked old and tawdry. Travers and the reporter went off to a Turkish bath, and the gentleman who held the watch, and who had been asleep for the last hour, dropped into a night-hawk and told the man to drive home. It was almost clear now and very cold, and Van Bibber determined to walk. He had the strange feeling one gets when one stays up until the sun rises, of having lost a day somewhere, and the dance he had attended a few hours before seemed to have come off long ago, and the fight in Jersey City was far back in the past.

The houses along the cross-street through which he

walked were as dead as so many blank walls, and only here and there a lace curtain waved out of the open window where some honest citizen was sleeping. The street was quite deserted; not even a cat or a policeman moved on it and Van Bibber's footsteps sounded brisk on the sidewalk. There was a great house at the corner of the avenue and the cross-street on which he was walking. The house faced the avenue and a stone wall ran back to the brown stone stable which opened on the side street. There was a door in this wall, and as Van Bibber approached it on his solitary walk it opened cautiously, and a man's head appeared in it for an instant and was withdrawn again like a flash, and the door snapped to. Van Bibber stopped and looked at the door and at the house and up and down the street. The house was tightly closed, as though someone was lying inside dead, and the streets were still empty.

Van Bibber could think of nothing in his appearance so dreadful as to frighten an honest man, so he decided the face he had had a glimpse of must belong to a dishonest one. It was none of his business, he assured himself, but it was curious, and he liked adventure, and he would have liked to prove his friend the reporter, who did not believe in adventure, in the wrong. So he approached the door silently, and jumped and caught at the top of the wall and stuck one foot on the handle of the door, and, with the other on the knocker, drew himself up and looked cautiously down on the other side. He had done this so lightly that the only noise he made was the rattle of the doorknob on which his foot had rested, and the man inside thought that the one outside was trying to open the door, and placed his shoulder to it and pressed against it heavily. Van Bibber, from his perch on the top of the wall, looked down directly on the other's head and shoulders. He could see the top of the man's head only two feet below, and he also saw that in one hand he held a revolver and that two bags filled with projecting articles of different sizes lay at his feet.

It did not need explanatory notes to tell Van Bibber that the man below had robbed the big house on the corner, and that if it had not been for his having passed when he did the burglar would have escaped with his treasure. His first thought was that he was not a policeman, and that a fight with a burglar was not in his line of life; and this was followed by the thought that though the gentleman who owned the property in the two bags was of no interest to him, he was, as a respectable member of society, more entitled to consideration than the man with the revolver.

The fact that he was now, whether he liked it or not, perched on the top of the wall like Humpty Dumpty, and that the burglar might see him and shoot him the next minute, had also an immediate influence on his movements. So he balanced himself cautiously and noiselessly and dropped upon the man's head and shoulders, bringing him down to the flagged walk with him and under him. The revolver went off once in the struggle, but before the burglar could know how or from where his assailant had come, Van Bibber was standing up over him and had driven his heel down on his hand and kicked the pistol out of his fingers. Then he stepped quickly to where it lay and picked it up and said, 'Now, if you try to get up I'll shoot at you.' He felt an unwarranted and ill-timedly humorous inclination to add, 'and I'll probably miss you,' but subdued it. The burglar, much to Van Bibber's astonishment, did not attempt to rise, but sat up with his hands locked across his knees and said: 'Shoot ahead. I'd a damned sight rather you would.'

His teeth were set and his face desperate and bitter, and hopeless to a degree of utter hopelessness that Van Bibber had never imagined.

'Go ahead,' reiterated the man, doggedly, 'I won't move. Shoot me.'

It was a most unpleasant situation. Van Bibber felt the pistol loosening in his hand, and he was conscious of a strong inclination to lay it down and ask the burglar to tell him all about it.

'You haven't got much heart,' said Van Bibber, finally. 'You're a pretty poor sort of a burglar, I should say.'

'What's the use?' said the man, fiercely. 'I won't go back – I won't go back there alive. I've served my time forever in that hole. If I have to go back again – s'help me if I don't do for a keeper and die for it. But I won't serve there no more.'

'Go back where?' asked Van Bibber, gently, and greatly interested; 'to prison?'

'To prison, yes!' cried the man, hoarsely: 'to a grave. That's where. Look at my face,' he said, 'and look at my hair. That ought to tell you where I've been. With all the colour gone out of my skin, and all the life out of my legs. You needn't be afraid of me. I couldn't hurt you if I wanted to. I'm a skeleton and a baby, I am. I couldn't kill a cat. And now you're going to send me back again for another lifetime. For twenty years, this time, into that cold, forsaken hole, and after I done my time so well and worked so hard.' Van Bibber shifted the pistol from one hand to the other and eyed his prisoner doubtfully.

'How long have you been out?' he asked, seating himself on the steps of the kitchen and holding the revolver between his knees. The sun was driving the morning mist away, and he had forgotten the cold.

'I got out yesterday,' said the man.

Van Bibber glanced at the bags and lifted the revolver. 'You didn't waste much time,' he said.

'No,' answered the man, sullenly, 'no, I didn't, I knew this place and I wanted money to get West to my folks, and the Society said I'd have to wait until I earned it, and I couldn't wait. I haven't seen my wife for seven years, nor my daughter. Seven years, young man; think of that – seven years. Do you know how long that is? Seven years without seeing your wife or your child! And they're straight people, they are,' he added, hastily. 'My wife moved West after I was put away and took another name, and my girl never knew nothing of me. She thinks I'm away at sea. I was to join 'em. That was the plan. I was to join 'em, and I thought I could lift enough here to get the fare, and now,' he added, dropping his face in his hands, 'I've got to go back. And I had meant to live straight after I got West – God help me, but I did! Not that it makes much difference now. An' I don't care whether you believe it or not neither,' he added, fiercely.

'I didn't say whether I believed it or not,' answered Van Bibber, with grave consideration.

He eyed the man for a brief space without speaking, and the burglar looked back at him, doggedly and defiantly, and with not the faintest suggestion of hope in his eyes, or of appeal for mercy. Perhaps it was because of this fact, or perhaps it was the wife and child that moved Van Bibber, but whatever his motives were, he acted on them promptly. 'I suppose, though,' he said, as though speaking to himself, 'that I ought to give you up.'

'I'll never go back alive,' said the burglar, quietly.

'Well, that's bad, too,' said Van Bibber. 'Of course I don't know whether you're lying or not, and as to your meaning to live honestly, I very much doubt it; but I'll give you a ticket to wherever your wife is, and I'll see you on the train. And you can get off at the next station and rob my house to-morrow night, if you feel that way about it. Throw those bags inside that door where the servant will see them before the milkman does, and walk on out ahead of me, and keep your hands in your pockets, and don't try to run. I have your pistol, you know.'

The man placed the bags inside the kitchen door; and, with a doubtful look at his custodian, stepped out into the street, and walked, as he was directed to do, toward the Grand Central station. Van Bibber kept just behind him, and kept turning the question over in his mind as to what he ought to do. He felt very guilty as he passed each policeman, but he recovered himself when he thought of the wife and child who lived in the West, and who were 'straight.'

'Where to?' asked Van Bibber, as he stood at the ticket-office window. 'Helena, Montana,' answered the man with, for the first time, a look of relief. Van Bibber bought the ticket and handed it to the burglar. 'I suppose you know,' he said, 'that you can sell that at a place down-town for half the money.' 'Yes, I know that,' said the burglar. There was a half-hour before the train left, and Van Bibber took his charge into the restaurant and watched him eat everything placed before him, with his eyes glancing all the while to the right or left. Then Van Bibber gave him some money and told him to write to him, and shook hands with him. The man nodded eagerly and pulled off his hat as the car drew out of the station; and Van Bibber came down-town again with the shop-girls and clerks going to work still wondering if he had done the right thing.

He went to his rooms and changed his clothes, took a cold bath, and crossed over to Delmonico's for his breakfast, and, while the waiter laid the cloth in the café, glanced at the headings in one of the papers. He scanned first with polite interest the account of the dance on the night previous and noticed his name among those present. With greater interest he read of the fight between 'Dutchy' Mack and the 'Black Diamond,' and then he read carefully how 'Abe' Hubbard, alias 'Jimmie the Gent,' a burglar, had broken jail in New Jersey, and had been traced to New York. There was a description of the man, and Van Bibber breathed quickly as he read it. 'The detectives have a clue to his whereabouts,' the account said; 'if he is still in the city they are confident of recapturing him. But they fear that the same friends who helped him to break jail will probably assist him from the country or to get out West.'

'They may do that,' murmured Van Bibber to himself, with a smile of grim contentment; 'they probably will.'

Then he said to the waiter, 'Oh, I don't know. Some bacon and eggs and green things and coffee.'

Oscar Wilde 1854–1900

Oscar Fingall O'Flahertie Wills Wilde was born in Dublin in 1854. He was educated at Trinity College, Dublin, and Magdalen College, Oxford, where he showed himself to be a brilliant scholar and a great wit. He kept people entertained with his stories which were so interesting they could 'charm toothache away'. 'He had one of the most alluring voices that I have listened to, round and soft and full of variety of expression and the cleverness of his remarks received added value from his manner of delivering them,' said Lillie Langtry, a famous English actress and a friend of the Prince of Wales.

At first Wilde wrote little, but was a great performer and went on tour of the United States and Canada, making a name for himself as a poet and art lecturer with an extravagant taste in clothes. With his marriage to Constance and the birth of two sons Wilde needed to earn money and became editor of the magazine *Woman's World* from 1887–1889. He also wrote down many of the stories which had begun life as oral tales and went on to write highly successful plays such as *The Importance of Being Earnest*.

At the height of his success Wilde was involved in a court case over a homosexual affair with Lord Alfred Douglas. Wilde was found guilty and given a sentence of two years' hard labour. After his release from prison he lived in France, physically and psychologically broken. His final work was the powerful poem about capital punishment, *The Ballad of Reading Gaol*. Wilde died in Paris in November 1900 quipping, 'If another century began and I was still alive it really would be more than the English could stand'.

The Nightingale and the Rose comes from the collection of stories for children, *The Happy Prince and Other Tales* (1888). Wilde used the form of the fairy tale to reflect on modern life and to debate ideas. So the story *The Nightingale and the Rose* deals not only with the nature of romance and true love, but also with art and the sacrifice of the artist. Wilde commented, 'The nightingale is the true lover, if there is one. She, at least, is Romance and the student and the girl are, like most of us, unworthy of Romance. So at least it seems to me but I like to fancy there may be many meanings in the tale . . .'

The Nightingale and the Rose

Oscar Wilde

'She said that she would dance with me if I brought her red roses,' cried the young Student; 'but in all my garden there is no red rose.'

From her nest in the holm-oak tree the Nightingale heard him, and she looked out through the leaves, and wondered.

'No red rose in all my garden!' he cried, and his beautiful eyes filled with tears. 'Ah, on what little things does happiness depend! I have read all that the wise men have written, and all the secrets of philosophy are mine, yet for want of a red rose is my life made wretched.'

'Here at last is a true lover,' said the Nightingale. 'Night after night have I sung of him though I knew him not: night after night have I told his story to the stars, and now I see him. His hair is dark as the hyacinth-blossom, and his lips are red as the rose of his desire; but passion has made his face like pale ivory, and sorrow has set her seal upon his brow.'

'The Prince gives a ball to-morrow night,' murmured the young Student, 'and my love will be of the company. If I bring her a red rose she will dance with me till dawn. If I bring her a red rose, I shall hold her in my arms, and she will lean her head upon my shoulder, and her hand will be clasped in mine. But there is no red rose in my garden, so I shall sit lonely, and she will pass me by. She will have no heed of me, and my heart will break.'

'Here indeed is the true lover,' said the Nightingale. 'What I sing of, he suffers: what is joy to me, to him is pain. Surely Love is a wonderful thing. It is more precious than emeralds, and dearer than fine opals. Pearls and pomegranates cannot buy it, nor is it set forth in the market-place. It may not be purchased of the merchants, nor can it be weighed out in the balance for gold.'

'The musicians will sit in their gallery,' said the young Student, 'and play upon their stringed instruments, and my love will dance to the sound of the harp and the violin. She will dance so lightly that her feet will not touch the floor, and the courtiers in their gay dresses will throng round her. But with me she will not dance, for I have no red rose to give her;' and he flung himself down on the grass, and buried his face in his hands, and wept.

'Why is he weeping?' asked a little Green Lizard, as he ran past him with his tail in the air.

'Why, indeed?' said a Butterfly, who was fluttering about after a sunbeam.

'Why, indeed?' whispered a Daisy to his neighbour, in a soft, low voice.

'He is weeping for a red rose,' said the Nightingale.

'For a red rose!' they cried; 'how very ridiculous!' and the little Lizard, who was something of a cynic, laughed outright.

But the Nightingale understood the secret of the Student's sorrow, and she sat silent in the oak-tree, and thought about the mystery of Love.

Suddenly she spread her brown wings for flight, and soared into the air. She passed through the grove like a shadow, and like a shadow she sailed across the garden.

In the centre of the grass-plot was standing a beautiful Rose-tree, and when she saw it, she flew over to it, and lit upon a spray.

'Give me a red rose,' she cried, 'and I will sing you my sweetest song.'

But the Tree shook its head.

'My roses are white,' it answered; 'as white as the foam of the sea, and whiter than the snow upon the mountain. But go to my brother who grows round the old sun-dial, and perhaps he will give you what you want.'

So the Nightingale flew over to the Rose-tree that was growing round the old sun-dial.

'Give me a red rose,' she cried, 'and I will sing you my sweetest song.'

But the Tree shook its head.

'My roses are yellow,' it answered; 'as yellow as the hair of the mermaiden who sits upon an amber throne, and yellower than the daffodil that blooms in the meadow before the mower comes with his scythe. But go to my brother who grows beneath the Student's window, and perhaps he will give you what you want.'

So the Nightingale flew over to the Rose-tree that was growing beneath the Student's window.

'Give me a red rose,' she cried, 'and I will sing you my sweetest song.'

But the Tree shook its head.

'My roses are red,' it answered, 'as red as the feet of the dove, and redder than the great fans of coral that wave and wave in the ocean-cavern. But the winter has chilled my veins, and the frost has nipped my buds, and the storm has broken my branches, and I shall have no roses at all this year.'

'One red rose is all I want,' cried the Nightingale, 'only one red rose! Is there no way by which I can get it?'

'There is a way,' answered the Tree; 'but it is so terrible that I dare not tell it to you.'

'Tell it to me,' said the Nightingale, 'I am not afraid.'

'If you want a red rose,' said the Tree, 'you must build it out of music by moonlight, and stain it with your own heart's-blood. You must sing to me with your breast against a thorn. All night long you must sing to me, and the thorn must pierce your heart, and your life-blood must flow into my veins, and become mine.'

'Death is a great price to pay for a red rose,' cried the Nightingale, 'and Life is very dear to all. It is pleasant to sit in the green wood, and to watch the Sun in his chariot of gold, and the Moon in her chariot of pearl. Sweet is the scent of the hawthorn, and sweet are the bluebells that hide in the valley, and the heather that blows on the hill. Yet Love is better than Life, and what is the heart of a bird compared to the heart of a man?'

So she spread her brown wings for flight, and soared into the air. She swept over the garden like a shadow, and like a shadow she sailed through the grove.

The young Student was still lying on the grass, where

she had left him, and the tears were not yet dry in his beautiful eyes.

'Be happy,' cried the Nightingale, 'be happy; you shall have your red rose. I will build it out of music by moonlight, and stain it with my own heart's-blood. All that I ask of you in return is that you will be a true lover, for Love is wiser than Philosophy, though she is wise, and mightier than Power, though he is mighty. Flame-coloured are his wings, and coloured like flame is his body. His lips are sweet as honey, and his breath is like frankincense.'

The Student looked up from the grass, and listened, but he could not understand what the Nightingale was saying to him, for he only knew the things that are written down in books.

But the Oak-tree understood, and felt sad, for he was very fond of the little Nightingale who had built her nest in his branches.

'Sing me one last song,' he whispered; 'I shall feel very lonely when you are gone.'

So the Nightingale sang to the Oak-tree, and her voice was like water bubbling from a silver jar.

When she had finished her song the Student got up, and pulled a note-book and a lead-pencil out of his pocket.

'She has form,' he said to himself, as he walked away through the grove – 'that cannot be denied to her; but has she got feeling? I am afraid not. In fact, she is like most artists; she is all style, without any sincerity. She would not sacrifice herself for others. She thinks merely of music, and everybody knows that the arts are selfish. Still, it must be admitted that she has some beautiful notes in her voice. What a pity it is that they do not mean anything, or do any practical good.' And he went into his room, and lay down on his little pallet-bed, and began to think of his love; and, after a time, he fell asleep.

And when the Moon shone in the heavens the Nightingale flew to the Rose-tree, and set her breast against the thorn. All night long she sang with her breast against the thorn, and the cold crystal Moon leaned down and listened. All night long she sang, and the thorn went deeper and deeper into her breast, and her life-blood ebbed away from her.

She sang first of the birth of love in the heart of a boy and a girl. And on the topmost spray of the Rose-tree there blossomed a marvellous rose, petal following petal, as song followed song. Pale was it, at first, as the mist that hangs over the river – pale as the feet of the morning, and silver as the wings of the dawn. As the shadow of a rose in a mirror of silver, as the shadow of a rose in a water-pool, so was the rose that blossomed on the topmost spray of the Tree.

But the Tree cried to the Nightingale to press closer against the thorn. 'Press closer, little Nightingale,' cried the Tree, 'or the Day will come before the rose is finished.'

So the Nightingale pressed closer against the thorn, and louder and louder grew her song, for she sang of the birth of passion in the soul of a man and a maid.

And a delicate flush of pink came into the leaves of the rose, like the flush in the face of the bridegroom when he kisses the lips of the bride. But the thorn had not yet reached her heart, so the rose's heart remained white, for only a Nightingale's heart's-blood can crimson the heart of a rose.

And the Tree cried to the Nightingale to press closer against the thorn. 'Press closer, little Nightingale,' cried the Tree, 'or the Day will come before the rose is finished.'

So the Nightingale pressed closer against the thorn, and the thorn touched her heart, and a fierce pang of pain shot through her. Bitter, bitter was the pain, and wilder and wilder grew her song, for she sang of the Love that is perfected by Death, of the Love that dies not in the tomb.

And that marvellous rose became crimson, like the rose of the eastern sky. Crimson was the girdle of petals, and crimson as a ruby was the heart.

But the Nightingale's voice grew fainter, and her little wings began to beat, and a film came over her eyes. Fainter and fainter grew her song, and she felt something choking her in her throat.

Then she gave one last burst of music. The white Moon heard it, and she forgot the dawn, and lingered on in the sky. The red rose heard it, and it trembled all over with ecstasy, and opened its petals to the cold morning air. Echo bore it to her purple cavern in the hills, and woke the sleeping shepherds from their dreams. It floated through the reeds of the river, and they carried its message to the sea.

'Look, look!' cried the Tree, 'the rose is finished now;' but the Nightingale made no answer, for she was lying dead in the long grass, with the thorn in her heart.

And at noon the Student opened his window and looked out.

'Why, what a wonderful piece of luck!' he cried; 'here is a red rose! I have never seen any rose like it in all my life. It is so beautiful that I am sure it has a long Latin name;' and he leaned down and plucked it.

Then he put on his hat, and ran up to the Professor's house with the rose in his hand.

The daughter of the Professor was sitting in the doorway winding blue silk on a reel, and her little dog was lying at her feet.

'You said that you would dance with me if I brought you a red rose,' cried the Student. 'Here is the reddest rose in all the world. You will wear it to-night next your heart, and as we dance together it will tell you how I love you.'

But the girl frowned.

'I am afraid it will not go with my dress,' she answered; 'and, besides, the Chamberlain's nephew has sent me some real jewels, and everybody knows that jewels cost far more than flowers.'

'Well, upon my word, you are very ungrateful,' said the Student angrily; and he threw the rose into the street, where it fell into the gutter, and a cart-wheel went over it.

'Ungrateful!' said the girl. 'I tell you what, you are very rude; and, after all, who are you? Only a Student. Why, I don't believe you have even got silver buckles to your shoes as the Chamberlain's nephew has;' and she got up from her chair and went into the house.

'What a silly thing Love is,' said the Student as he walked away. 'It is not half as useful as Logic, for it does not prove anything, and it is always telling one of things that are not going to happen, and making one believe things that are not true. In fact, it is quite unpractical, and, as in this age to be practical is everything, I shall go back to Philosophy and study Metaphysics.'

So he returned to his room and pulled out a great dusty book, and began to read.

Olive Schreiner 1855–1920

Olive Schreiner was born in 1855 in Cape Province, the ninth child of a German father and a British mother. Her parents had emigrated to South Africa to work as Christian missionaries. Olive Schreiner grew up in an isolated, poverty stricken home in which five of her brothers and sisters died in infancy. She lived in an environment full of racial tension and strict Christian morality with parents who believed in the value of corporal punishment. She educated herself, with the help of her mother, by reading as widely as she could. By the age of 17 she was an atheist, a socialist, a pacifist and a feminist.

Olive Schreiner wrote three novels – the first, *Undine*, when she was a teenager. She took the manuscripts of all three with her when she moved to England at the age of 26. Her second novel *The Story of an African Farm* was published in 1883 under the pseudonym of Ralph Iron. The story of a woman's battle to preserve her own identity on an isolated South African farm, the novel drew upon many of the problems and ideas that Olive Schreiner had encountered herself. *The Story of an African Farm* was a huge success; by 1900 one hundred thousand copies had been sold in three continents. She continued to work on her third novel, *From Man to Man*, at various points throughout her life. It was eventually published in 1926, six years after her death.

In 1894 Olive Schreiner married. In 1895 her only child, a daughter, died a few hours after birth. She lived in South Africa and in England, suffering from long periods of ill health associated with her asthma. But she was a fighter all her life, in her political activity and in her writing. After 1883 she wrote mainly non-fiction: pamphlets, articles and books arguing for the causes she believed in. She fought for women's rights – to vote, and to be treated equally in domestic and economic matters. In Southern African politics she supported the Afrikaners against the British, opposed the imperialism of Cecil Rhodes and argued forcefully for the rights of the black majority.

The Woman's Rose is an example of her working in a

quieter, more reflective mode but, as a story about the value and difficulties of women's friendship, it reflects concerns that were of central importance to Olive Schreiner's life.

The Woman's Rose

Olive Schreiner

I have an old, brown, carved box; the lid is broken and tied with a string. In it I keep little squares of paper, with hair inside, and a little picture which hung over my brother's bed when we were children, and other things as small. I have in it a rose. Other women also have such boxes where they keep such trifles, but no one has my rose.

When my eye is dim, and my heart grows faint, and my faith in woman flickers, and her present is an agony to me, and her future a despair, the scent of that dead rose, withered for twelve years, comes back to me. I know there will be spring; as surely as the birds know it when they see above the snow two tiny, quivering green leaves. Spring cannot fail us.

There were other flowers in the box once: a bunch of white acacia flowers, gathered by the strong hand of a man, as we passed down a village street on a sultry afternoon, when it had rained, and the drops fell on us from the leaves of the acacia trees. The flowers were damp; they made mildew marks on the paper I folded them in. After many years I threw them away. There is nothing of them left in the box now, but a faint, strong smell of dried acacia, that recalls that sultry summer afternoon; but the rose is in the box still.

It is many years ago now; I was a girl of fifteen, and I went to visit in a small up-country town. It was young in those days, and two days' journey from the nearest village; the population consisted mainly of men. A few were married, and had their wives and children, but most were single. There was only one young girl there when I came. She was about seventeen, fair, and rather fully-fleshed; she had large dreamy blue eyes, and wavy light hair; full, rather heavy lips, until she smiled; then her face broke into dimples, and all her white teeth shone. The hotel-keeper may have had a daughter, and the farmer in the outskirts had two, but we never saw them. She reigned alone. All the men worshipped her. She was the only woman they had to think of. They talked of her on the 'stoep', at the market, at the hotel; they watched for her at street corners; they hated the men she bowed to or walked with down the street. They brought flowers to the front door; they offered her their horses; they begged her to marry them when they dared. Partly, there was something noble and heroic in this devotion of men to the best woman they knew; partly there was something natural in it, that these men, shut off from the world, should pour at the feet of one woman the worship that otherwise would have been given to twenty; and partly there was something mean in their envy of one another. If she had raised her little finger, I suppose, she might have married any one out of twenty of them.

Then I came. I do not think I was prettier; I do not think I was so pretty as she was. I was certainly not as handsome. But I was vital, and I was new, and she was old – they all forsook her and followed me. They worshipped me. It was to my door that the flowers came; it was I had twenty horses offered me when I could only ride one; it was for me they waited at street corners; it was what I said and did that they talked of. Partly I liked it. I had lived alone all my life; no one ever had told me I was beautiful and a woman. I believed them. I did not know it was simply a fashion, which one man had set and the rest followed unreasoningly. I liked them to ask me to marry them, and to say, No. I despised them. The mother heart had not swelled in me yet; I did not know all men were my children, as the large woman knows when her heart is grown. I was too small to be tender. I liked my power. I was like a child with a new whip, which it goes about cracking everywhere, not caring against what. I could not wind it up and put it away. Men were curious creatures, who liked me, I could never tell why. Only one thing took from my pleasure; I could not bear that they had deserted her for me. I liked her great dreamy blue eyes, I liked her slow walk and drawl; when I saw her sitting among men, she seemed to me much too good to be among them; I would have given all their compliments if she would once have smiled at me as she smiled at them, with all her face breaking into radiance, with her dimples and flashing teeth. But I knew it never could be; I felt sure she hated me; that she wished I was dead; that she wished I had never come to the village. She did not know, when we went out riding, and a man who had always ridden beside her came to ride beside me, that I sent him away; that once when a man thought to win my favour by ridiculing her slow drawl before me I turned on him so fiercely that he never dared come before me again. I knew she knew that at the hotel men had made a bet as to which was the prettier, she or I, and had asked each man who came in, and that the one who had staked on me won. I hated them for it, but I would not let her see that I cared about what she felt towards me.

She and I never spoke to each other.

If we met in the village street we bowed and passed on; when we shook hands we did so silently, and did not look at each other. But I thought she felt my presence in a room just as I felt hers.

At last the time for my going came. I was to leave the next day. Someone I knew gave a party in my honour, to which all the village was invited.

It was midwinter. There was nothing in the gardens but a few dahlias and chrysanthemums, and I suppose that for two hundred miles round there was not a rose to be bought for love or money. Only in the garden of a friend of mine, in a sunny corner between the oven and the brick wall, there was a rose tree growing which had on it one bud. It was white, and it had been promised to the fair-haired girl to wear at the party.

The evening came; when I arrived and went to the waiting-room, to take off my mantle, I found the girl there already. She was dressed in pure white, with her great white arms and shoulders showing, and her bright hair glittering in the candlelight, and the white rose fastened at her breast. She looked like a queen. I said 'Good-evening,' and turned away quickly to the glass to arrange my old black scarf across my old black dress.

Then I felt a hand touch my hair.

'Stand still,' she said.

I looked in the glass. She had taken the white rose from her breast, and was fastening it in my hair.

'How nice dark hair is; it sets off flowers so.' She stepped back and looked at me. 'It looks much better there!'

I turned round.

'You are so beautiful to me,' I said.

'Y-e-s,' she said, with her slow Colonial drawl; 'I'm so glad.'

We stood looking at each other.

Then they came in and swept us away to dance. All the evening we did not come near to each other. Only once, as she passed, she smiled at me.

The next morning I left the town.

I never saw her again.

Years afterwards I heard she had married and gone to America; it may or may not be so – but the rose – the rose is in the box still! When my faith in woman grows dim, and it seems that for want of love and magnanimity she can play no part in any future heaven; then the scent of that small withered thing comes back – spring cannot fail us.

Charlotte Perkins Gilman 1860–1935

When Charlotte Perkins Gilman died in 1935 she left a huge legacy of writing – a volume of poetry (and hundreds of uncollected poems), nearly 200 short stories, 9 novels and an enormous number of articles and essays. As a young woman she had determined that her life would be one of independence and work, and that work should be about improving the world. Running through all of her writing is a deep seated concern about injustice and inequality; throughout her life she worked for the trade union movement, for the cause of women's suffrage and for more equal treatment of men and women in all aspects of their home and working lives.

Born Charlotte Anna Perkins in Connecticut, USA, in 1860, she was brought up by her mother after her father left the family. She studied at art school and for a time made her living by designing greetings cards. In January 1882 she met Charles Walter Stetson, an artist well known for his charm and good looks. For some years she was unsure about marrying him. She worried particularly about whether she would be able to match what was expected of a wife and mother in American society at that time, and how she would be able to continue the political and artistic work she considered so important. In May 1884 she married and later gave birth to a daughter.

From the start of her marriage Charlotte Stetson was prone to depression; after Katharine's birth she fell into so deep a post-natal depression that her husband insisted upon consulting a doctor famous for his treatment of women's nervous disorders. This doctor prescribed a 'rest cure': 'Live as domestic a life as possible . . . Lie down an hour after each meal. Have but two hours intellectual life a day. And never touch pen, brush, or pencil as long as you live.'

This supposed 'cure' almost drove Charlotte Stetson mad. Her depression arose, at least in part, from her sense of being restricted and unable to work creatively. The 'treatment' made things so bad that she felt that she never fully recovered and that she was left to live 'a crippled life'. She wrote *The Yellow Wallpaper* in 1892 to show just how destructive such attitudes to women could be. The story was shocking to many readers at the time. It was rediscovered in the late 1960s and 70s and remains one of her most popular and widely read works – not least because many modern readers feel that they can find parallels with women's lives today.

Charlotte Stetson separated from her husband and devoted herself to her work. She wrote and lectured, shared the care of her daughter and looked after her mother until her death. In 1900 she re-married – George Gilman, a first cousin. In 1932 Charlotte Perkins Gilman found that she had an inoperable cancer; in 1935, when the end was in sight, she committed suicide preferring as she explained in her last note 'chloroform to cancer'.

The Yellow Wallpaper

Charlotte Perkins Gilman

It is very seldom that mere ordinary people like John and myself secure ancestral halls for the summer.

A colonial mansion, a hereditary estate, I would say a haunted house and reach the height of romantic felicity – but that would be asking too much of fate!

Still I will proudly declare that there is something queer about it.

Else, why should it be let so cheaply? And why have stood so long untenanted?

John laughs at me, of course, but one expects that.

John is practical in the extreme. He has no patience with faith, an intense horror of superstition, and he scoffs openly at any talk of things not to be felt and seen and put down in figures.

John is a physician,* and *perhaps* – (I would not say it to a living soul, of course, but this is dead paper and a great relief to my mind) – *perhaps* that is one reason I do not get well faster.

You see, he does not believe I am sick! And what can one do?

If a physician of high standing, and one's own husband, assures friends and relatives that there is really nothing the matter with one but temporary nervous depression – a slight hysterical tendency – what is one to do?

My brother is also a physician, and also of high standing, and he says the same thing.

So I take phosphates or phosphites – whichever it is – and tonics, and air and exercise, and journeys, and am absolutely forbidden to 'work' until I am well again.

* doctor

Personally, I disagree with their ideas.

Personally, I believe that congenial work, with excitement and change, would do me good.

But what is one to do?

I did write for a while in spite of them; but it *does* exhaust me a good deal – having to be so sly about it, or else meet with heavy opposition.

I sometimes fancy that in my condition, if I had less opposition and more society and stimulus – but John says the very worst thing I can do is to think about my condition, and I confess it always makes me feel bad.

So I will let it alone and talk about the house.

The most beautiful place! It is quite alone, standing well back from the road, quite three miles from the village. It makes me think of English places that you read about, for there are hedges and walls and gates that lock, and lots of separate little houses for the gardeners and people.

There is a *delicious* garden! I never saw such a garden – large and shady, full of box-bordered paths, and lined with long grape-covered arbors with seats under them.

There were greenhouses, but they are all broken now.

There was some legal trouble, I believe, something about the heirs and co-heirs; anyhow, the place has been empty for years.

That spoils my ghostliness, I am afraid, but I don't care – there is something strange about the house – I can feel it.

I even said so to John one moonlight evening, but he said what I felt was a draught, and shut the window.

I get unreasonably angry with John sometimes. I'm sure I never used to be so sensitive. I think it is due to this nervous condition.

But John says if I feel so I shall neglect proper self-control; so I take pains to control myself – before him, at least, and that makes me very tired.

I don't like our room a bit. I wanted one downstairs that opened onto the piazza and had roses all over the window, and such pretty old-fashioned chintz hangings! But John would not hear of it.

He said there was only one window and not room for two beds, and no near room for him if he took another.

He is very careful and loving, and hardly lets me stir without special direction.

I have a schedule prescription for each hour in the day; he takes all care from me, and so I feel basely ungrateful not to value it more.

He said he came here solely on my account, that I was to have perfect rest and all the air I could get. 'Your exercise depends on your strength, my dear,' said he, 'and your food somewhat on your appetite; but air you can absorb all the time.' So we took the nursery at the top of the house.

It is a big, airy room, the whole floor nearly, with windows that look all ways, and air and sunshine galore. It was a nursery first, and then playroom and gymnasium, I should judge, for the windows are barred for little children, and there are rings and things in the walls.

The paint and paper look as if a boys' school had used it. It is stripped off – the paper – in great patches all around the head of my bed, about as far as I can reach, and in a great place on the other side of the room low down. I never saw a worse paper in my life. One of those sprawling, flamboyant patterns committing every artistic sin.

It is dull enough to confuse the eye in following, pronounced enough constantly to irritate and provoke study, and when you follow the lame uncertain curves for a little distance they suddenly commit suicide – plunge off at outrageous angles, destroy themselves in unheard-of contradictions.

The color is repellent, almost revolting: a smouldering unclean yellow, strangely faded by the slow-turning sunlight. It is a dull yet lurid orange in some places, a sickly sulphur tint in others.

No wonder the children hated it! I should hate it myself if I had to live in this room long.

There comes John, and I must put this away – he hates to have me write a word.

We have been here two weeks, and I haven't felt like writing before, since that first day.

I am sitting by the window now, up in this atrocious

nursery, and there is nothing to hinder my writing as much as I please, save lack of strength.

John is away all day, and even some nights when his cases are serious.

I am glad my case is not serious!

But these nervous troubles are dreadfully depressing.

John does not know how much I really suffer. He knows there is no reason to suffer, and that satisfies him.

Of course it is only nervousness. It does weigh on me so not to do my duty in any way!

I meant to be such a help to John, such a real rest and comfort, and here I am a comparative burden already!

Nobody would believe what an effort it is to do what little I am able – to dress and entertain, and order things.

It is fortunate Mary is so good with the baby. Such a dear baby!

And yet I *cannot* be with him, it makes me so nervous.

I suppose John never was nervous in his life. He laughs at me so about this wallpaper!

At first he meant to repaper the room, but afterward he said that I was letting it get the better of me, and that nothing was worse for a nervous patient than to give way to such fancies.

He said that after the wallpaper was changed it would be the heavy bedstead, and then the barred windows, and then that gate at the head of the stairs, and so on.

'You know the place is doing you good,' he said, 'and really, dear, I don't care to renovate the house just for a three months' rental.'

'Then do let us go downstairs,' I said. 'There are such pretty rooms there.'

Then he took me in his arms and called me a blessed little goose, and said he would go down cellar, if I wished, and have it whitewashed into the bargain.

But he is right enough about the beds and windows and things.

It is as airy and comfortable a room as anyone need wish, and, of course, I would not be so silly as to make him uncomfortable just for a whim.

I'm really getting quite fond of the big room, all but that horrid paper.

Out of one window I can see the garden – those mysterious deep-shaded arbors, the riotous old-fashioned flowers, and bushes and gnarly trees.

Out of another I get a lovely view of the bay and a little private wharf belonging to the estate. There is a beautiful shaded lane that runs down there from the house. I always fancy I see people walking in these numerous paths and arbors, but John has cautioned me not to give way to fancy in the least. He says that with my imaginative power and habit of story-making, a nervous weakness like mine is sure to lead to all manner of excited fancies, and that I ought to use my will and good sense to check the tendency. So I try.

I think sometimes that if I were only well enough to write a little it would relieve the press of ideas and rest me.

But I find I get pretty tired when I try.

It is so discouraging not to have any advice and companionship about my work. When I get really well, John says we will ask Cousin Henry and Julia down for a long visit; but he says he would as soon put fireworks in my pillow-case as to let me have those stimulating people about now.

I wish I could get well faster.

But I must not think about that. This paper looks to me as if it *knew* what a vicious influence it had!

There is a recurrent spot where the pattern lolls like a broken neck and two bulbous eyes stare at you upside down.

I get positively angry with the impertinence of it and the everlastingness. Up and down and sideways they crawl, and those absurd unblinking eyes are everywhere. There is one place where two breadths didn't match, and the eyes go all up and down the line, one a little higher than the other.

I never saw so much expression in an inanimate thing before, and we all know how much expression they have! I used to lie awake as a child and get more entertainment and terror out of blank walls and plain furniture than most children could find in a toy-store.

I remember what a kindly wink the knobs of our big old

bureau used to have, and there was one chair that always seemed like a strong friend.

I used to feel that if any of the other things looked too fierce I could always hop into that chair and be safe.

The furniture in this room is no worse than inharmonious, however, for we had to bring it all from downstairs. I suppose when this was used as a playroom they had to take the nursery things out, and no wonder! I never saw such ravages as the children have made here.

The wallpaper, as I said before, is torn off in spots, and it sticketh closer than a brother – they must have had perseverance as well as hatred.

Then the floor is scratched and gouged and splintered, the plaster itself is dug out here and there, and this great heavy bed, which is all we found in the room, looks as if it had been through the wars.

But I don't mind it a bit – only the paper.

There comes John's sister. Such a dear girl as she is, and so careful of me! I must not let her find me writing.

She is a perfect and enthusiastic housekeeper, and hopes for no better profession. I verily believe she thinks it is the writing which made me sick!

But I can write when she is out, and see her a long way off from these windows.

There is one that commands the road, a lovely shaded winding road, and one that just looks off over the country. A lovely country, too, full of great elms and velvet meadows.

This wallpaper has a kind of sub-pattern in a different shade, a particularly irritating one, for you can only see it in certain lights, and not clearly then.

But in the places where it isn't faded and where the sun is just so – I can see a strange, provoking, formless sort of figure that seems to skulk about behind that silly and conspicuous front design.

There's sister on the stairs!

Well, the Fourth of July is over! The people are all gone, and I am tired out. John thought it might do me good to see a little company, so we just had Mother and Nellie and the children down for a week.

Of course I didn't do a thing. Jennie sees to everything now.

But it tired me all the same.

John says if I don't pick up faster he shall send me to Weir Mitchell in the fall.

But I don't want to go there at all. I had a friend who was in his hands once, and she says he is just like John and my brother, only more so!

Besides, it is such an undertaking to go so far.

I don't feel as if it was worthwhile to turn my hand over for anything, and I'm getting dreadfully fretful and querulous.

I cry at nothing, and cry most of the time.

Of course I don't when John is here, or anybody else, but when I am alone.

And I am alone a good deal just now. John is kept in town very often by serious cases, and Jennie is good and lets me alone when I want her to.

So I walk a little in the garden or down that lovely lane, sit on the porch under the roses, and lie down up here a good deal.

I'm getting really fond of the room in spite of the wallpaper. Perhaps *because* of the wallpaper.

It dwells on my mind so!

I lie here on this great immovable bed – it is nailed down, I believe – and follow that pattern about by the hour. It is as good as gymnastics, I assure you. I start, we'll say, at the bottom, down in the corner over there where it has not been touched, and I determine for the thousandth time that I *will* follow that pointless pattern to some sort of a conclusion.

I know a little of the principle of design, and I know this thing was not arranged on any laws of radiation, or alternation, or repetition, or symmetry, or anything else that I ever heard of.

It is repeated, of course, by the breadths, but not otherwise.

Looked at in one way, each breadth stands alone; the bloated curves and flourishes – a kind of 'debased Romanesque' with delirium tremens – go waddling up and down in isolated columns of fatuity.

But, on the other hand, they connect diagonally, and the sprawling outlines run off in great slanting waves of optic horror, like a lot of wallowing sea-weeds in full chase.

The whole thing goes horizontally, too, at least it seems so, and I exhaust myself trying to distinguish the order of its going in that direction.

They have used a horizontal breadth for a frieze, and that adds wonderfully to the confusion.

There is one end of the room where it is almost intact, and there, when the crosslights fade and the low sun shines directly upon it, I can almost fancy radiation after all – the interminable grotesque seems to form around a common center and rush off in headlong plunges of equal distraction.

It makes me tired to follow it. I will take a nap, I guess.

I don't know why I should write this.

I don't want to.

I don't feel able.

And I know John would think it absurd. But I *must* say what I feel and think in some way – it is such a relief!

But the effort is getting to be greater than the relief.

Half the time now I am awfully lazy, and lie down ever so much. John says I mustn't lose my strength, and has me take cod liver oil and lots of tonics and things, to say nothing of ale and wine and rare meat.

Dear John! He loves me very dearly, and hates to have me sick. I tried to have a real earnest reasonable talk with him the other day, and tell him how I wish he would let me go and make a visit to Cousin Henry and Julia.

But he said I wasn't able to go, nor able to stand it after I got there; and I did not make out a very good case for myself, for I was crying before I had finished.

It is getting to be a great effort for me to think straight. Just this nervous weakness, I suppose.

And dear John gathered me up in his arms, and just carried me upstairs and laid me on the bed, and sat by me and read to me till it tired my head.

He said I was his darling and his comfort and all he had, and that I must take care of myself for his sake, and keep well.

He says no one but myself can help me out of it, that I must use my will and self-control and not let any silly fancies run away with me.

There's one comfort – the baby is well and happy, and does not have to occupy this nursery with the horrid wallpaper.

If we had not used it, that blessed child would have! What a fortunate escape! Why, I wouldn't have a child of mine, an impressionable little thing, live in such a room for worlds.

I never thought of it before, but it is lucky that John kept me here after all; I can stand it so much easier than a baby, you see.

Of course I never mention it to them any more – I am too wise – but I keep watch for it all the same.

There are things in that wallpaper that nobody knows about but me, or ever will.

Behind that outside pattern the dim shapes get clearer every day.

It is always the same shape, only very numerous.

And it is like a woman stooping down and creeping about behind that pattern. I don't like it a bit. I wonder – I begin to think – I wish John would take me away from here!

It is so hard to talk with John about my case, because he is so wise, and because he loves me so.

But I tried it last night.

It was moonlight. The moon shines in all around just as the sun does.

I hate to see it sometimes, it creeps so slowly, and always comes in by one window or another.

John was asleep and I hated to waken him, so I kept still and watched the moonlight on that undulating wallpaper till I felt creepy.

The faint figure behind seemed to shake the pattern, just as if she wanted to get out.

I got up softly and went to feel and see if the paper *did* move, and when I came back John was awake.

'What is it, little girl?' he said. 'Don't go walking about like that – you'll get cold.'

I thought it was a good time to talk, so I told him that I

really was not gaining here, and that I wished he would take me away.

'Why, darling!' said he. 'Our lease will be up in three weeks, and I can't see how to leave before.

'The repairs are not done at home, and I cannot possibly leave town just now. Of course, if you were in any danger, I could and would, but you really are better, dear, whether you can see it or not. I am a doctor, dear, and I know. You are gaining flesh and color, your appetite is better, I feel really much easier about you.'

'I don't weigh a bit more,' said I, 'nor as much; and my appetite may be better in the evening when you are here but it is worse in the morning when you are away!'

'Bless her little heart!' said he with a big hug. 'She shall be as sick as she pleases! But now let's improve the shining hours by going to sleep, and talk about it in the morning!'

'And you won't go away?' I asked gloomily.

'Why, how can I, dear? It is only three weeks more and then we will take a nice little trip of a few days while Jennie is getting the house ready. Really, dear, you are better!'

'Better in body perhaps – ' I began, and stopped short, for he sat up straight and looked at me with such a stern, reproachful look that I could not say another word.

'My darling,' said he, 'I beg of you, for my sake and for our child's sake, as well as for your own, that you will never for one instant let that idea enter your mind! There is nothing so dangerous, so fascinating, to a temperament like yours. It is a false and foolish fancy. Can you not trust me as a physician when I tell you so?'

So of course I said no more on that score, and we went to sleep before long. He thought I was asleep first, but I wasn't, and lay there for hours trying to decide whether that front pattern and the back pattern really did move together or separately.

On a pattern like this, by daylight, there is a lack of sequence, a defiance of law, that is a constant irritant to a normal mind.

The color is hideous enough, and unreliable enough, and infuriating enough, but the pattern is torturing.

You think you have mastered it, but just as you get well

under way in following, it turns a back-somersault and there you are. It slaps you in the face, knocks you down, and tramples upon you. It is like a bad dream.

The outside pattern is a florid arabesque, reminding one of a fungus. If you can imagine a toadstool in joints, an interminable string of toadstools, budding and sprouting in endless convolutions – why, that is something like it.

That is, sometimes!

There is one marked peculiarity about this paper, a thing nobody seems to notice but myself, and that is that it changes as the light changes.

When the sun shoots in through the east window – I always watch for that first long, straight ray – it changes so quickly that I never can quite believe it.

That is why I watch it always.

By moonlight – the moon shines in all night when there is a moon – I wouldn't know it was the same paper.

At night in any kind of light, in twilight, candlelight, lamplight, and worst of all by moonlight, it becomes bars! The outside patterns, I mean, and the woman behind it as plain as can be.

I didn't realize for a long time what the thing was that showed behind, that dim sub-pattern, but now I am quite sure it is a woman.

By daylight she is subdued, quiet. I fancy it is the pattern that keeps her so still. It is so puzzling. It keeps me quiet by the hour.

I lie down ever so much now. John says it is good for me, and to sleep all I can.

Indeed he started the habit by making me lie down for an hour after each meal.

It is a very bad habit, I am convinced, for you see, I don't sleep.

And that cultivates deceit, for I don't tell them I'm awake – oh, no!

The fact is I am getting a little afraid of John.

He seems very queer sometimes, and even Jennie has an inexplicable look.

It strikes me occasionally, just as a scientific hypothesis, that perhaps it is the paper!

I have watched John when he did not know I was

looking, and come into the room suddenly on the most innocent excuses, and I've caught him several times *looking at the paper!* And Jennie too. I caught Jennie with her hand on it once.

She didn't know I was in the room, and when I asked her in a quiet, a very quiet voice, with the most restrained manner possible, what she was doing with the paper, she turned around as if she had been caught stealing, and looked quite angry – asked me why I should frighten her so!

Then she said that the paper stained everything it touched, that she had found yellow smooches on all my clothes and John's and she wished we would be more careful!

Did not that sound innocent? But I know she was studying that pattern, and I am determined that nobody shall find it out but myself!

Life is very much more exciting now than it used to be. You see, I have something more to expect, to look forward to, to watch. I really do eat better, and am more quiet than I was.

John is so pleased to see me improve! He laughed a little the other day, and said I seemed to be flourishing in spite of my wallpaper.

I turned it off with a laugh. I had no intention of telling him it was *because* of the wallpaper – he would make fun of me. He might even want to take me away.

I don't want to leave now until I have found it out. There is a week more, and I think that will be enough.

I'm feeling so much better!

I don't sleep much at night, for it is so interesting to watch developments; but I sleep a good deal during the daytime.

In the daytime it is tiresome and perplexing.

There are always new shoots on the fungus, and new shades of yellow all over it. I cannot keep count of them, though I have tried conscientiously.

It is the strangest yellow, that wallpaper! It makes me think of all the yellow things I ever saw – not beautiful ones like buttercups, but old, foul, bad yellow things.

But there is something else about that paper – the smell! I noticed it the moment we came into the room, but with so much air and sun it was not bad. Now we have had a week of fog and rain, and whether the windows are open or not, the smell is here.

It creeps all over the house.

I find it hovering in the dining-room, skulking in the parlor, hiding in the hall, lying in wait for me on the stairs.

It gets into my hair.

Even when I go to ride, if I turn my head suddenly and surprise it – there is that smell!

Such a peculiar odor, too! I have spent hours in trying to analyze it, to find what it smelled like.

It is not bad – at first – and very gentle, but quite the subtlest, most enduring odor I ever met.

In this damp weather it is awful. I wake up in the night and find it hanging over me.

It used to disturb me at first. I thought seriously of burning the house – to reach the smell.

But now I am used to it. The only thing I can think of that it is like is the *color* of the paper! A yellow smell.

There is a very funny mark on this wall, low down, near the mopboard. A streak that runs round the room. It goes behind every piece of furniture, except the bed, a long, straight, even *smooch*, as if it had been rubbed over and over.

I wonder how it was done and who did it, and what they did it for. Round and round and round – round and round and round – it makes me dizzy!

I really have discovered something at last.

Through watching so much at night, when it changes so, I have finally found out.

The front pattern *does* move – and no wonder! The woman behind shakes it!

Sometimes I think there are a great many women behind, and sometimes only one, and she crawls around fast, and her crawling shakes it all over.

Then in the very bright spots she keeps still, and in the very shady spots she just takes hold of the bars and shakes them hard.

And she is all the time trying to climb through. But nobody could climb through that pattern – it strangles so; I think that is why it has so many heads.

They get through, and then the pattern strangles them off and turns them upside down, and makes their eyes white!

If those heads were covered or taken off it would not be half so bad.

I think that woman gets out in the daytime!

And I'll tell you why – privately – I've seen her!

I can see her out of every one of my windows!

It is the same woman, I know, for she is always creeping, and most women do not creep by daylight.

I see her in that long shaded lane, creeping up and down. I see her in those dark grape arbors, creeping all around the garden.

I see her on that long road under the trees, creeping along, and when a carriage comes she hides under the blackberry vines.

I don't blame her a bit. It must be very humiliating to be caught creeping by daylight!

I always lock the door when I creep by daylight. I can't do it at night, for I know John would suspect something at once.

And John is so queer now that I don't want to irritate him. I wish he would take another room! Besides, I don't want anybody to get that woman out at night but myself.

I often wonder if I could see her out of all the windows at once.

But, turn as fast as I can, I can only see out of one at one time.

And though I always see her, she *may* be able to creep faster than I can turn! I have watched her sometimes away off in the open country, creeping as fast as a cloud shadow in a wind.

If only that top pattern could be gotten off from the under one! I mean to try it, little by little.

I have found out another funny thing, but I shan't tell it this time! It does not do to trust people too much.

There are only two more days to get this paper off, and I

believe John is beginning to notice. I don't like the look in his eyes.

And I heard him ask Jennie a lot of professional questions about me. She had a very good report to give.

She said I slept a good deal in the daytime.

John knows I don't sleep very well at night, for all I'm so quiet!

He asked me all sorts of questions, too, and pretended to be very loving and kind.

As if I couldn't see through him!

Still, I don't wonder he acts so, sleeping under this paper for three months.

It only interests me, but I feel sure John and Jennie are affected by it.

Hurrah! This is the last day, but it is enough. John is to stay in town over night, and won't be out until this evening.

Jennie wanted to sleep with me – the sly thing; but I told her I should undoubtedly rest better for a night all alone.

That was clever, for really I wasn't alone a bit! As soon as it was moonlight and that poor thing began to crawl and shake the pattern, I got up and ran to help her.

I pulled and she shook. I shook and she pulled, and before morning we had peeled off yards of that paper.

A strip about as high as my head and half around the room.

And then when the sun came and that awful pattern began to laugh at me, I declared I would finish it today!

We go away tomorrow, and they are moving all my furniture down again to leave things as they were before.

Jennie looked at the wall in amazement, but I told her merrily that I did it out of pure spite at the vicious thing.

She laughed and said she wouldn't mind doing it herself, but I must not get tired.

How she betrayed herself that time!

But I am here, and no person touches this paper but Me – not *alive!*

She tried to get me out of the room – it was too patent! But I said it was so quiet and empty and clean now that I believed I would lie down again and sleep all I could, and not to wake me even for dinner – I would call when I woke.

So now she is gone, and the servants are gone, and the things are gone, and there is nothing left but that great bedstead nailed down, with the canvas mattress we found on it.

We shall sleep downstairs tonight, and take the boat home tomorrow.

I quite enjoy the room, now it is bare again.

How those children did tear about here!

This bedstead is fairly gnawed!

But I must get to work.

I have locked the door and thrown the key down into the front path.

I don't want to go out, and I don't want to have anybody come in, till John comes.

I want to astonish him.

I've got a rope up here that even Jennie did not find. If that woman does get out, and tries to get away, I can tie her!

But I forgot I could not reach far without anything to stand on!

This bed will *not* move!

I tried to lift and push it until I was lame, and then I got so angry I bit off a little piece at one corner – but it hurt my teeth.

Then I peeled off all the paper I could reach standing on the floor. It sticks horribly and the pattern just enjoys it! All those strangled heads and bulbous eyes and waddling fungus growths just shriek with derision!

I am getting angry enough to do something desperate. To jump out of the window would be admirable exercise, but the bars are too strong even to try.

Besides I wouldn't do it. Of course not. I know well enough that a step like that is improper and might be misconstrued.

I don't like to *look* out of the windows even – there are so many of those creeping women, and they creep so fast.

I wonder if they all come out of that wallpaper as I did?

But I am securely fastened now by my well-hidden rope – you don't get *me* out in the road there!

I suppose I shall have to get back behind the pattern when it comes night, and that is hard!

It is so pleasant to be out in this great room and creep around as I please!

I don't want to go outside. I won't, even if Jennie asks me to.

For outside you have to creep on the ground, and everything is green instead of yellow.

But here I can creep smoothly on the floor, and my shoulder just fits in that long smooch around the wall, so I cannot lose my way.

Why, there's John at the door!

It is no use, young man, you can't open it!

How he does call and pound!

Now he's crying to Jennie for an axe.

It would be a shame to break down that beautiful door!

'John, dear!' said I in the gentlest voice. 'The key is down by the front steps, under a plantain leaf!'

That silenced him for a few moments.

Then he said, very quietly indeed, 'Open the door, my darling!'

'I can't,' said I. 'The key is down by the front door under a plantain leaf!' And then I said it again, several times, very gently and slowly, and said it so often that he had to go and see, and he got it of course, and came in. He stopped short by the door.

'What is the matter?' he cried. 'For God's sake, what are you doing!'

I kept on creeping just the same, but I looked at him over my shoulder.

'I've got out at last,' said I, 'in spite of you and Jane. And I've pulled off most of the paper, so you can't put me back!'

Now why should that man have fainted? But he did, and right across my path by the wall, so that I had to creep over him every time!

Maxim Gorky 1868–1936

Maxim Gorky was the pen name of the Russian writer Alexei Maximovich Peshkov, who was born in Nizhny Novgorod in 1868. At the age of three Gorky's father died of cholera which he had caught from his young son. Although Gorky was seriously ill he recovered, but his mother blamed him for his father's death and he was sent away to live with his grandparents. His mother died when he was eleven and at twelve Gorky ran away to lead a wandering, poverty-stricken life amongst the poorest people in society. It was these experiences, and his determination that society should change, which gave Gorky much of the starkly realist subject matter of his writing.

He began writing for newspapers in 1892 and adopted his pen name 'Gorky'. Translated from the Russian this means '*wretched*' relating to the harsh conditions of his childhood, and '*bitter*' describing the flavour of his work. He went on to write a number of short stories and a series of autobiographical works for which he is best known – *My Childhood* (1913), *My Apprenticeship* (1916) and *My Universities* (1923). In 1917 Gorky welcomed the Russian revolution, but left the Soviet Union for health reasons and lived in Capri until 1928. When he returned home he was received with enthusiasm and became an important literary figure.

The story *Twenty-six Men and a Girl* (1899) deals with one of the constant themes of Gorky's work: can people live poverty-stricken tough lives without a comforting illusion to sustain them? And if they create these illusions does it stop them fighting against the terrible conditions they live in? Basing the story on his own experience of work in a bakery in Kazan he describes how the men are trapped like prisoners by the dreadful conditions of their work. Their one consolation is the presence of a pretty sixteen-year-old girl Tanya who works upstairs and is the only person who takes an interest in them. They love and idealise her 'because there was no-one else to love.'

Twenty-six Men and a Girl

Maxim Gorky

There were twenty-six of us – twenty-six living machines – incarcerated from morning to night in a damp basement-room, making dough for pretzels and cracknels. The windows of this room gave out on to a large pit sunk into the ground and lined with bricks which had grown green from mould; the window frames were barred on the outside with close-meshed grilles and and the sunlight was unable to penetrate the flour-covered glass. Our boss had barred off the windows to prevent us giving any of his bread to the beggars and those comrades of ours who were unemployed and starving. He called us crooks and gave us putrid offal instead of meat for dinner.

Life in this stone box with its low, heavy ceiling, covered in cobwebs and blackened from smoke, was stifling and cramped. Within these thick, dirt-stained walls, rotten with mildew, we led a wretched and miserable existence. We got up at five in the morning, still tired, and by six o'clock, dulled and indifferent, we were sitting at the table making pretzels from dough which others had been preparing while we were asleep. And the whole day, until ten in the evening, some of us sat at the table untwisting the soft dough and swaying backwards and forwards to prevent stiffness, while the others mixed the flour and water. All day long the boiling water in the cauldron where the pretzels were cooked bubbled away to itself in sorrowful meditation, and the baker's shovel rasped in hasty anger against the bottom of the oven, as he tossed the slippery pieces of boiled dough on to the hot bricks. From morning till night the wood burnt in one section of the oven, the red flames casting a flickering shadow onto the wall of the bakery, as if in silent mockery of its inhabitants. The huge oven was like the misshapen head of some mythical monster, seemingly rising out of the floor and opening its huge fiery jaws, exhaling flames and viewing our endless toil through the two sunken air-vents in its forehead. These two deep hollows were like eyes – a monster's pitiless, dispassionate eyes with a persistently veiled expression, as if they had grown tired of looking at slaves, despising them with the cold scorn of wisdom and expecting nothing human from them.

Day in, day out, covered with flour dust and the dirt which we brought in on our boots, in the fetid, suffocating atmosphere we untwisted dough and made pretzels, moistening them with the sweat of our brows, and we hated our work with a deep loathing. We never ate anything that we ourselves had made, preferring black bread to the pretzels. Sitting at a long table opposite each other – nine against nine – we worked mechanically away with our fingers and hands for hours on end, and we had grown so used to our work that we no longer even watched what we were doing. We knew each other's faces so well that every wrinkle was familiar. There was nothing to talk about and we had become accustomed to the silence, broken only by the sound of cursing, for you can always find a reason to curse someone, especially if he is a mate. But this didn't happen very often; how can someone be to blame if he's half-dead, turned to stone, his feelings crushed by the burden of work? But silence is painful and terrifying only for those who have already said everything and who have nothing left to say; but to those who have not yet begun to talk, silence comes easily and simply.

Sometimes, however, we would sing, and our singing would generally start in the following way: as we sat there working, one of us would suddenly sigh deeply like a weary horse, and start quietly to sing one of those long-drawn-out songs whose plaintively caressing melody always has the effect of lightening the singer's heart. At first we would listen in silence to his solitary voice, and his song would melt and die away in the heavy basement ceiling, like the flickering of a bonfire in the steppes* on a raw autumn

* plains

evening when the grey sky hangs over the earth like a leaden roof. Then someone else would take up the song and the two voices would hover wistfully and gently in the suffocating air of our crowded dungeon. Suddenly several voices would join in all at once and the song would roar and foam like an ocean wave, increasing in volume until it seemed that it would tear asunder the damp, thick walls of our stone prison.

All twenty-six of us would sing and the room would be filled with the sound of loud, confident voices. The room was too small to contain such a sound: it crashed against the stone walls, its cries and groans evoking a dull, throbbing anguish in our hearts, and re-opening old wounds. The singers would sigh, deeply and heavily. Every so often someone would abruptly stop singing and sit for a long time listening to the rest and then his voice would once more merge into the general wave of sound. Some would sing with their eyes closed, interspersing their singing with loud, anguished exclamations, imagining perhaps this broad and dense wave of sound to be a sunlit road leading into the distance, a wide road along which they were walking . . .

And all the time the stove crackled, the baker's shovel rasped against the bricks, the water bubbled in the boiler and the reflection of the fire played on the wall in silent mockery . . . and we would use the words of the song to express our dulled feeling of despair, the overbearing anguish of living people who have been deprived of the sun, the anguish of slaves. Thus the twenty-six of us lived, in the basement of a large stone house, and our lives were so oppressed that it seemed as if we were carrying all three storeys of this house on our shoulders.

But there was something else that brought joy into our lives, apart from the singing, something that we had come to love and look forward to and which perhaps took the place of the sun in our hearts. On the second floor of the house there was a workshop where gold-lined silk threads were made. Here, among the girls who worked there, lived a sixteen-year-old girl who did the cleaning and tidying, called Tanya. Every morning a small pink face with laughing blue eyes would press up against the little window let into the door of our room and a ringing, affectionate voice would call out:

'Hey, convicts, let's have the pretzels then!'

At the sound of this clear voice we would all turn round and look happily and good-naturedly at the innocent face of the young girl, smiling so sweetly at us. We used to love seeing her nose, pressed up against the glass and her small, white teeth showing between her pink, smiling lips. We would rush to open the door for her, jostling each other, and she would come in looking so sweet and happy, holding up her apron, and stand in front of us, her head a little to one side and smiling all the while. Her long, thick, chestnut-coloured hair fell in a plait over her shoulder and lay on her breast. Ugly, dirty, ignorant, we would stand there and look up at her – the doorway was four steps higher than the floor of our room – we would look at her, our heads turned upwards, saying good morning to her and using words which came to us only when we talked to her. Our voices became more gentle, our jokes less harsh. We were quite different when she was with us. The baker would take a shovelful of newly baked, especially crunchy pretzels and skilfully toss them up into Tanya's apron.

'Watch out for the boss!' we would warn her. She would give a sly little laugh and, bidding us good-bye, would vanish as quickly as a mouse.

And that was all . . . But long after she had gone, we would talk happily about her amongst ourselves, saying the same things as the day before and the day before that, because both she and we, and everything around us, were just the same as they had always been. Life for those whose circumstances never change is agonizing and very difficult: the longer they live, the more agonizing such circumstances become, if their spirits are not broken altogether. When we spoke about women, the coarse and indecent expressions we used would sometimes revolt even us; the women we knew, of course, perhaps deserved no better. But we never spoke in this way about Tanya and not only did we never touch her, but we never made any suggestive remarks in her presence. Perhaps this may have been because she never stayed with us for long: she would appear fleetingly before our eyes like a falling star and then disappear. Or perhaps it was because she was small and very beautiful and anything beautiful always commands the respect of even uncultured people. And also, even although our forced labour had reduced us to the level of beasts of the field, we nonetheless were still human beings and, like all human beings, we were unable to live without worshipping at least something. We had nobody who was better than she was, nobody, apart from her, who paid any attention to us living down in the basement, although the house was inhabited by scores of people. And finally, probably most importantly, we all considered her to be ours, someone who existed only because of our pretzels; we considered it our duty to provide her with pretzels hot from the oven, and this became for us an act of daily sacrifice to our idol, an almost sacred ritual which bound us more closely to her with each passing day. Apart from the pretzels we would also give Tanya a lot of advice, telling her to dress more warmly, not to run down the stairs too fast or to carry bundles of wood which were too heavy for her. She would listen to our advice with a smile and laughed in reply, but she never obeyed us and we were not in the least offended; we wanted only to show that we cared about her.

Often she would ask us to do something for her, such as to open the heavy door into the cellar for her, or to chop some wood. We would do these things for her, and anything else she wanted, eagerly and with a sense even of pride.

But when one day one of us asked her to darn his shirt, the only one he had, she snorted scornfully, saying:

'I'm not doing that! Whatever next!'

We burst out laughing at the naïve fellow and never asked her to do anything for us again. We loved her, and that's all there is to be said. People always need somebody to love, even though sometimes such a love can oppress, sully or poison a fellow human being's life, for they can love someone without respecting them. We loved Tanya, we had to love her, because there was no one else to love.

Sometimes one of us would suddenly begin to ask:

'What do we want to pay this girl so much attention for? What's so special about her? We fuss over her too much!'

But anybody who took it into his head to say such things

we cut quickly and sharply down to size, for we needed an object for our love. We had found something, which for each of us had to remain for ever sacred, and anybody who denied us this was our enemy. Perhaps we loved something that was not truly good, but there were after all twenty-six of us and so we always wanted to see that the rest of us held sacred what was most precious to each of our hearts.

Our love is no less oppressive than hatred, and this is perhaps precisely why some proud souls among us maintain that our hatred is more flattering than love . . . But, if that is so, why do they not run away from us?

Apart from the pretzel bakehouse our boss also owned an ordinary bakery. It was situated in the same house, separated from our dungeon only by a wall; but the bakers there, of which there were four, kept apart from us, considering their work purer than ours and therefore considering themselves better than us. They never visited us in our room and would laugh disdainfully at us whenever they met us outside. Neither would we go into their room: the boss had forbidden us to do so in case we should start stealing the buns. We had no love for those bakers because we envied them: their work was easier than ours, they were paid better, fed better, their room was spacious and light and we found them all repulsively clean and healthy. We all had yellowish-grey faces, three of us had syphilis, some had skin disease, and one was completely crippled with rheumatism. At holidays and in their free time the bakers would dress up in jackets and squeaky boots, a couple of them owned accordions, and they would all go for a walk in the municipal park, whereas we wore filthy rags, with down-at-heel shoes or bast-sandals* on our feet, and the police would not allow us in the park – how then could we like them?

One day we learnt that one of them had gone on the bottle, for which the boss had sacked him and taken on someone else – a soldier who went around in a satin waistcoat with a watch on a gold chain. We were very anxious to catch sight of this splendid fellow and we

* rope-sandals

started to take turns to run out into the yard in the hope of seeing him.

But he came to our room himself. Kicking the door open, he stood in the doorway, saying with a smile:

'God bless you! Greetings, lads!'

The frosty air, rushing into the room in thick, billowing clouds, swirled about his feet while he stood there in the doorway looking down at us, his large, yellow teeth gleaming under his fair, smartly twirled moustache. His waistcoat was indeed something out of the ordinary – dark blue, embroidered with flowers, it seemed to shine all over. Its buttons were of little red stones, and there was a watch-chain too . . .

He was handsome, this soldier, tall, healthy-looking with ruddy cheeks and a friendly cheerful expression in his large, clear eyes. On his head he wore a white starched cap and from under his spotlessly clean apron peeped the pointed toes of a pair of fashionable, highly polished boots.

Our baker politely asked him to close the door; he did so unhurriedly and started to question us about the boss. Interrupting each other, we informed him that our boss was a cunning rogue, a crook, a scoundrel and a tyrant – and anything else that could and should have been said about him, but which is impossible to repeat here. The soldier listened to us, twirling his moustache, and looking at us with a friendly, open expression.

'You've got a lot of girls here,' he suddenly said.

Some of us laughed deferentially, others put on honeyed expressions and someone told him that there were nine girls altogether.

'Do you make use of them?' the soldier asked with a wink.

Once again we laughed, but this time rather quietly and sheepishly. Many of us would like to have shown the soldier that we too shared his devil-may-care attitude, but not one of us was able to do so. Someone confessed as much:

'That's not really our line . . .' he said.

'Hm, yes, I see: it can't be easy for you!' said the soldier confidently, examining us carefully. 'You're a bit . . . well . . . I mean, you haven't got the right manner or look, as it were. And women like the way a man looks, above all! They like a man with a real body, with everything in its place. And they respect strength, too, men with arms like this . . .!'

The soldier drew his right hand out of his pocket and showed us his bare arm, with his shirt-sleeve rolled up to the elbow. It was a white, strong arm, covered in glistening, golden hair.

'Legs, chest – everything should be firm and strong. And then again, a man should be well dressed, as the fashion demands. Women go for me in a big way. I don't have to egg them on at all; I have them hanging on my neck, five at a time, of their own accord.'

He sat down on a bag of flour where he stayed for a long time, telling us how much the women loved him and how royally he treated them. Then he left and when the door had creaked shut behind him we remained silent for a long while thinking about him and what he had told us. And then we all suddenly began to talk, and it became clear at once that he had made a good impression on all of us. Such an unassuming, splendid fellow – he had simply come in, sat down and started talking. Nobody came in to see us, nobody talked with us in such a friendly way. And so we continued to talk about him and discuss his future exploits with the sewing girls. Whenever these girls met us in the yard they would either haughtily purse their lips and deliberately avoid us or walk directly at us as if we were not there at all. But we always continued to admire them, whether we saw them in the yard or walking past our windows, dressed, in winter, in their best hats and fur coats and, in summer, in flowery hats and carrying gaily coloured parasols. And yet, amongst ourselves, we always referred to these girls in terms which, had they heard us, would have infuriated them with a sense of shame and outrage.

'Let's hope he doesn't get his hands on our Tanya!' the baker suddenly said anxiously.

We all fell silent, struck by these words. We had somehow forgotten about Tanya: it was as if the soldier's well-set, handsome figure had quite driven her out of our minds. Then a noisy argument developed, some of us saying that

Tanya would never allow it to happen, others that she would not be able to resist the soldier's advances, and still others maintaining that they would break the soldier's ribs if he began to force his attentions on her. In the end we all decided to watch both of them and to warn Tanya to be wary of him. On this note the argument ended.

About a month passed; the soldier baked his rolls, went about with the sewing girls and frequently dropped in to see us, but said nothing about any conquests, simply twirling his moustache and smacking his lips.

Each morning Tanya came for her pretzels, as happy, sweet and kind to us as ever. We tried to start talking to her about the soldier, but she called him a 'goggle-eyed calf' and other such funny nicknames, which set our minds at rest. We were proud of our Tanya when we saw the other girls crowding round the soldier. Her attitude towards him lifted all our hearts somehow, and, as if guided by this attitude, we ourselves began to adopt a rather disparaging approach to him. But we loved her all the more and greeted her every morning even more happily and good-naturedly than before.

But one day the soldier came to see us somewhat the worse for drink. He sat down and began to laugh, and when we asked him what was so funny he said:

'A couple of them have been fighting over me – Lida and Grushka. You should have seen them clawing at each other! Ha, ha! One got the other by the hair, threw her down on the floor of the passage and sat on her! Ha, ha, ha! They scratched and tore at each other's faces . . . what a laugh! Why can't women fight fairly, without scratching each other, eh?'

He sat there on the bench, radiating health, freshness and happiness, and roaring with laughter. We were silent. This time he made an unpleasant impression on us.

'I don't half have luck with the girls, eh? What a laugh! One wink and they're ready, by God!'

He raised his white hands glistening with hair and then slapped them down on his knees. Then he looked at us with an expression of surprised pleasure on his face as if he were genuinely puzzled at his own success with women. His plump, red face gleamed with happiness and self-satisfaction and all the time he smacked his lips in enjoyment.

Suddenly our baker thrust his shovel noisily and angrily along the bottom of the oven and remarked ironically:

'It doesn't take very much strength to chop down a tiny fir tree, but just try chopping down a full-grown pine.'

'What do you mean? Are you talking to me?' asked the soldier.

'Yes, I am . . .'

'What about me?'

'It's nothing . . . just a slip of the tongue.'

'Hey, no, hold on! What are you talking about? What pine?'

Our baker did not reply but just went on shovelling away, tossing the half-cooked pretzels into the stove, fishing out the ones that were done and tossing them noisily onto the floor where the young lads threaded them on to bast strings. He seemed to have forgotten about the soldier and what he had been saying to him. But the soldier suddenly became very agitated. He stood up and went to the oven, risking a collision with the end of the shovel, which was flashing feverishly through the air.

'Now tell me who she is. You've offended me, insulted me with what you've just said. I could get any one of them I wanted to!'

It was true: he did seem genuinely put out. It seemed that it was only from his prowess as a seducer of women that he derived his self-respect; this was perhaps the only vital quality he possessed and without it he could not consider himself a living person.

For there are people whose sickness of mind or body is the most precious trait they possess. They spend their whole lives nurturing it and live only for it. They suffer terribly because of it and complain about it to other pepole and so draw attention to themselves. And in this way they elicit other people's sympathy but, apart from this, they have nothing. If you were to deprive them of this illness by curing it, they would be unhappy because they would have lost their one resource in life and would be left quite empty. A man's life can sometimes become so wretched that he can be driven against his will to cherish his particular vice and to live by it alone; it could be said, too, that it is often boredom which turns people to depravity.

Anyway the soldier took umbrage, went up to our baker and started shouting at him.

'You just tell me who you mean?'

'You want me to tell you?' said the baker, suddenly turning to face him.

'Well?'

'You know Tanya?'

'Well?'

'Well, that's the one! Just try her . . .'

'Me?'

'Yes, you!'

'Tanya! Pah, that's nothing!'

'We'll see!'

'You'll see, all right! Ha!'

'She'll . . .'

'Give me a month!'

'You're just a windbag, soldier!'

'A fortnight! I'll show you! Tanya, you say? Pah!'

'Go on, get out. You're in my way!'

'A fortnight, that's all! You . . .'

'Get out, I say!'

And our baker, in a fit of fury, suddenly started brandishing his shovel. The soldier stepped back in astonishment, looked at us for a moment in silence, quietly and menacingly said, 'Right then!' and left the room.

During all this time we had stayed silent, engrossed in the argument. But when the soldier had gone there was an outburst of noise and animated conversation.

'You shouldn't have done that, Pavel!' someone shouted at the baker.

'You get on with your work!' the baker answered savagely.

We sensed that the soldier had been deeply wounded and that danger threatened Tanya, and yet at the same time we were all seized by a burning and pleasurable feeling of curiosity: what would happen? Would she be able to resist him? And almost everyone shouted with certainty:

'Our Tanya? She'll hold out! You can't get her just like that!'

We had a terrible longing to test the strength of our idol; we repeatedly assured ourselves that our idol would stand firm and emerge the victor from this encounter. And, finally, we began to feel that we had not incited the soldier enough, that he would forget about the argument and that we should wound his pride properly. From that day onwards our way of life changed into something we had never experienced before. We became especially tense and nervous, argued amongst ourselves for days on end, gaining, as it were, in intelligence and talking better and at greater length. It seemed to us that we were somehow gambling with the devil and that our stake was Tanya. And when we learnt from the bakers next door that the soldier had begun to 'go after our Tanya' we experienced a sort of delighted terror and we became so fascinated by it all that we did not even notice when our boss, taking advantage of our state, added an extra 500 pounds of dough to our day's quota. Our work, it seemed, no longer even tired us. Tanya's name was constantly on our lips, and we used to wait for her each morning with particular impatience. Sometimes we imagined that she would come, and that it wouldn't be the girl we knew, but a different Tanya.

However, we said nothing to her about the argument we had had. We put no questions to her and treated her as well and as affectionately as ever. But now our attitude contained a hint of something new, something which we had not felt before towards her, and this was a sharp curiosity, as sharp and as cold as a steel knife.

'The two weeks are up today, mates!' the baker announced one morning, as he set to work.

We were all well aware of this, without being reminded, but a thrill ran through us nonetheless.

'Look at her, when she comes,' said the baker. 'She'll be here in a minute.'

'Yes, but we won't know just by looking at her, surely,' someone exclaimed regretfully.

And once again a noisy, lively argument flared up among us. Today, at last, we would find out just how pure and chaste the vessel was into which we had poured all that was good in us. It was that morning for the first time we suddenly realized that we were indeed playing for high stakes and that this test of our idol's purity might destroy it in our eyes. Throughout the two weeks we had heard that the soldier had been persisently and relentlessly chasing Tanya, but why then had one of us not asked her what she thought? And she had continued coming to us punctually each morning for her pretzels and had been just the same as ever.

That morning, too, we soon heard her voice:

'Hey, convicts! Here I am!'

We rushed to let her in, and when she came into the room met her in unaccustomed silence. Our eyes fixed on her, we did not know what to say to her or what to ask her, but just stood before her in a dark, silent mass. She was clearly astonished by this unusual greeting and, as we watched, we suddenly saw her face grow pale and agitated. She started fidgeting and then asked in a subdued voice:

'What's the matter with you all?'

'What about you?' the baker snapped morosely, not taking his eyes off her.

'Me? What do you mean?'

'Ah, forget it . . .'

'Well, come on, be quick, let's have the pretzels.'

Never before had she tried to hasten us.

'What's the hurry?' asked the baker, standing quite motionless, his eyes still fixed on her.

She suddenly turned and disappeared through the door.

The baker took up his shovel and, turning to the oven, said calmly:

'Well, that's it, then. That soldier, the bastard!'

Jostling each other like a flock of sheep, we went to the table, silently sat down and apathetically started working. Soon one of us said:

'Maybe, after all, she didn't . . .'

'Tell us another one!' shouted the baker.

We all knew that he was a clever man, cleverer than the rest of us. And we all took this response as an indication of his certainty that the soldier had won . . . We felt an uneasy sadness.

The soldier came at twelve o'clock when we were eating. As always he had a clean, smart appearance and, as always, he looked us straight in the eyes. But we were too embarrassed to look at him.

'Well then, my dear sirs,' he said with an arrogant smirk. 'Would you like me to show you the stuff a soldier's made of? Come out into the passage then and look through the cracks, all right?'

We went out and, crowding together, squeezed up against the cracks in the wooden walls of the passage which led out into the yard. We did not have to wait long. Soon Tanya came into the yard walking quickly with an anxious expression, jumping over the puddles of melting snow and mud. She disappeared into the door leading down into the cellar. Then we saw the soldier strolling unhurriedly along, whistling, his hands in his pockets and his moustache quivering; he too disappeared into the cellar doorway.

It was raining and we watched the rain drops wrinkling the surface of the puddles. It was a raw, grey and extremely dreary day. Snow still lay on the rooftops, but on the ground dark patches of mud were beginning to appear, and even the snow on the roofs was stained a dark, muddy brown colour. The rain was falling slowly with a melancholy sound. For us, waiting there, it was cold and unpleasant.

First to emerge from the cellar was the soldier. He walked slowly across the yard, his moustache quivering, his hands in his pockets – just the same as ever.

And then Tanya appeared. Her eyes – her eyes were radiant with joy and happiness and her lips were smiling. She walked as though in a dream, swaying unsteadily.

Unable to restrain ourselves, we rushed at once to the door, dashed out into the yard and began to whistle and jeer at her loudly and viciously, like wild beasts.

She started when she saw us and stood as though rooted to the mud under her feet. We surrounded her and reviled her maliciously, without restraint, heaping obscenities on her.

We did this quietly and unhurriedly, seeing that she could not escape us, that we surrounded her and that we could jeer at her as much as we liked. She stood in the middle of us, turning her head from side to side, as she listened to our insults. And with ever increasing violence we bombarded her with the filth and venom of our words.

The colour drained from her face. Her blue eyes, which had a minute before been so happy, were now wide open, her breathing was laboured and her lips trembled.

But we stood in a ring round her and exacted our revenge, for she had robbed us. She had belonged to us, we had poured all that was good in us into her and, although this may well have been the crumbs of mere beggars, nevertheless there was only one of her while we were twenty-six, and so there was no pain we could inflict on her which was equal to her guilt! How we insulted her! She did not say a word, but just looked at us with wild eyes and trembled all over.

We laughed, roared and yelled . . . Other people ran over to join us, and one of us tugged at the sleeve of her jacket.

Suddenly her eyes flashed; she slowly raised her hands to her head and, smoothing her hair, said loudly but calmly straight to our faces:

'Ah, you miserable little convicts!'

And she walked straight at us, just like that, as if we were not there blocking her way. And, because of this, we made way for her.

When she had got out of our ring she, without turning round, said just as loudly but with an added note of contemptuous pride:

'You pigs . . . you brutes!'

And upright, beautiful, proud, she walked away.

And we were left standing in the middle of the yard, in the mud and the rain under the grey, sunless sky.

Then we too went silently back into our damp stone pit. As before, the sun never shone into our windows – and Tanya never came to us again!

Charles Dickens 1812–1870

Charles Dickens was born on the south coast of England, near Portsmouth, where his father was a Naval pay clerk. When he was three years old his family moved to Chatham in Kent and seven years later, to London. In London, the Dickens family were to fall upon extremely hard times and his father was actually imprisoned for debt in the notorious Marshalsea Prison – the memory of these times was to haunt Dickens for the rest of his life.

Because of poverty, the young Dickens was withdrawn from school and sent to work in a bleaching warehouse. He did manage to return to school briefly but left again at 15 to become first a clerk, then a short-hand reporter in the law courts.

In his early twenties he began to write a series of often humorous articles for a variety of magazines. They were very popular with readers and he was encouraged to continue writing. There followed a string of famous titles – *The Pickwick Papers, Oliver Twist, Great Expectations* – all of which were first published in instalments for various magazines and periodicals. Charles Dickens became a best seller.

In 1850 Dickens started his own weekly journal *Household Words*. He also began to devote more of his time to the public reading of his works, in both this country and North America. His readings were hugely successful affairs, often involving numerous dramatic presentations, but they were also physically exhausting. Dickens was to die suddenly in 1870 before reaching the age of sixty.

The Poor Relation's Story is taken from the special Christmas edition of *Household Words* for 1852. Brief in comparison to most of his work, the story is a good introduction to his writing; note for example the care taken over the names of his characters – Uncle Chill and Betsy Snap.

The Christmas stories were seen by Dickens as entertainments in the main, to be read aloud within the family circle. But *The Poor Relation's Story* is more than just an entertainment, as Dickens manages to cleverly interweave an edge of biting social comment. Dickens felt strongly, for obvious personal reasons, about the neglect of the poor and he regularly described himself as a 'Reformer – heart and soul'. Seen in this light, the revelation at the end of the story is particularly telling.

The Poor Relation's Story

Charles Dickens

CHARACTERS

Uncle Chill, *an avaricious, crabbed old man; uncle to Michael.*
Christiana, *an old sweetheart of Michael's.*
Little Frank, *a diffident boy; a cousin of Michael's.*
Michael, *the 'poor relation', and narrator of the story.*
Betsy Snap, *a withered old woman, Uncle Chill's servant.*
John Spatter, *Michael's clerk, afterwards his partner.*

He was very reluctant to take precedence of so many respected members of the family, by beginning the round of stories they were to relate as they sat in a goodly circle by the Christmas fire; and he modestly suggested that it would be more correct if 'John our esteemed host' (whose health he begged to drink) would have the kindness to begin. For as to himself, he said, he was so little used to lead the way that really – But as they all cried out here, that he must begin, and agreed with one voice that he might, could, would, and should begin, he left off rubbing his hands, and took his legs out from under his armchair, and did begin.

I have no doubt (said the poor relation) that I shall surprise the assembled members of our family, and particularly John our esteemed host to whom we are so much indebted for the great hospitality with which he has this day entertained us, by the confession I am going to make. But, if you do me the honour to be surprised at anything that falls from a person so unimportant in the family as I am, I can only say that I shall be scrupulously accurate in all I relate.

I am not what I am supposed to be. I am quite another thing. Perhaps before I go further, I had better glance at what I *am* supposed to be.

It is supposed, unless I mistake – the assembled members of our family will correct me if I do, which is very likely (here the poor relation looked mildly about him for contradiction); that I am nobody's enemy but my own. That I never met with any particular success in anything. That I failed in business because I was unbusiness-like and credulous – in not being prepared for the interested designs of my partner. That I failed in love, because I was ridiculously trustful – in thinking it impossible that Christiana could deceive me. That I failed in my expectations from my Uncle Chill, on account of not being as sharp as he could have wished in wordly matters. That, through life, I have been rather put upon and disappointed in a general way. That I am at present a bachelor of between fifty-nine and sixty years of age, living on a limited income in the form of a quarterly allowance, to which I see that John our esteemed host wishes me to make no further allusion.

The supposition as to my present pursuits and habits is the following effect.

I live in a lodging in the Clapham Road – a very clean back room, in a very respectable house – where I am expected not to be at home in the day-time, unless poorly; and which I usually leave in the morning at nine o'clock, on pretence of going to business. I take my breakfast – my roll and butter, and my half-pint of coffee – at the old-established coffee-shop near Westminster Bridge; and then I go into the City – I don't know why – and sit in Garraway's Coffee House, and on 'Change, and walk about, and look into a few offices and counting-houses where some of my relations or acquaintance are so good as to tolerate me, and where I stand by the fire if the weather happens to be cold. I get through the day in this way until five o'clock, and then I dine: at a cost, on the average, of one and threepence. Having still a little money to spend on my evening's entertainment, I look into the old-established coffee-shop as I go home, and take my cup of tea, and perhaps my bit of toast. So, as the large hand of the clock makes its way round to the morning hours again, I make my way round to the Clapham Road again, and go to bed when I get to my lodging – fire being expensive, and being objected to by the family on account of its giving trouble and making a dirt.

Sometimes, one of my relations or acquaintance is so obliging as to ask me to dinner. Those are holiday occasions, and then I generally walk in the Park. I am a solitary man, and seldom walk with anybody. Not that I am avoided because I am shabby; for I am not at all shabby, having always a good suit of black on (or rather Oxford mixture, which has the appearance of black and wears much better); but I have got into a habit of speaking low, and being rather silent, and my spirits are not high, and I am sensible that I am not an attractive companion.

The only exception to this general rule is the child of my first cousin, Little Frank. I have a particular affection for that child, and he takes very kindly to me. He is a diffident boy by nature; and in a crowd he is soon run over, as I may say, and forgotten. He and I, however, get on exceedingly well. I have a fancy that the poor child will in time succeed to my peculiar position in the family. We talk but little; still, we understand each other. We walk about, hand in hand; and without much speaking he knows what I mean, and I know what he means. When he was very little indeed, I used to take him to the windows of the toy-shops, and show him the toys inside. It is surprising how soon he found out that I would have made him a great many presents if I had been in circumstances to do it.

Little Frank and I go and look at the outside of the Monument – he is very fond of the Monument – and at the Bridges, and at all the sights that are free. On two of my birthdays, we have dined on à-la-mode beef, and gone at half-price to the play, and been deeply interested. I was once walking with him in Lombard Street, which we often visit on account of my having mentioned to him that there are great riches there – he is very fond of Lombard Street – when a gentleman said to me as he passed by, 'Sir, your little son has dropped his glove.' I assure you, if you will excuse my remarking on so trivial a circumstance, this accidental mention of the child as mine, quite touched my heart and brought the foolish tears into my eyes.

When Little Frank is sent to school in the country, I shall be very much at a loss what to do with myself, but I have the intention of walking down there once a month and seeing him on a half-holiday. I am told he will then be at play upon the Heath; and if my visits should be objected to, as unsettling the child, I can see him from a distance without his seeing me, and walk back again. His mother comes of a highly genteel family, and rather disapproves, I am aware, of our being too much together. I know that I am not calculated to improve his retiring disposition; but I think he would miss me beyond the feeling of the moment if we were wholly separated.

When I die in the Clapham Road, I shall not leave much more in this world than I shall take out of it; but, I happen to have a miniature of a bright-faced boy, with a curling head, and an open shirt-frill waving down his bosom (my mother had it taken for me, but I can't believe that it was ever like), which will be worth nothing to sell, and which I shall beg may be given to Frank. I have written my dear boy a little letter with it, in which I have told him that I felt very sorry to part from him, though bound to confess that I knew no reason why I should remain here. I have given him some short advice, the best of my power, to take warning of the consequences of being nobody's enemy but his own; and I have endeavoured to comfort him for what I fear he will consider a bereavement, by pointing out to him, that I was only a superfluous something to every one but him; and that having by some means failed to find a place in this great assembly, I am better out of it.

Such (said the poor relation, clearing his throat and beginning to speak a little louder) is the general impression about me. Now, it is a remarkable circumstance which forms the aim and purpose of my story, that this is all wrong. This is not my life, and these are not my habits. I do not even live in Clapham Road. Comparatively speaking, I am very seldom there. I reside, mostly, in a – I am almost ashamed to say the word, it sounds so full of pretension – in a Castle. I do not mean that it is an old baronial habitation, but still it is a building always known to every one by the name of a Castle. In it, I preserve the particulars of my history; they run thus:

It was when I first took John Spatter (who had been my clerk) into partnership, and when I was still a young man of not more than five-and-twenty, residing in the house of my uncle Chill, from whom I had considerable expectations, that I ventured to propose to Christiana. I had loved Christiana a long time. She was very beautiful, and very winning in all respects. I rather mistrusted her widowed mother, who I feared was of a plotting and mercenary turn of mind; but, I thought as well of her as I could, for Christiana's sake. I never had loved any one but Christiana, and she had been all the world, and O far more than all the world, to me, from our childhood!

Christiana accepted me with her mother's consent, and I was rendered very happy indeed. My life at my uncle Chill's was of a spare dull kind, and my garret chamber was as dull, and bare, and cold, as an upper prison room in some stern northern fortress. But, having Christiana's love, I wanted nothing upon earth. I would not have changed my lot with any human being.

Avarice was, unhappily, my uncle Chill's master-vice. Though he was rich, he pinched, and scraped, and clutched, and lived miserably. As Christiana had no fortune, I was for some time a little fearful of confessing our engagement to him; but, at length I wrote him a letter, saying how it all truly was. I put it into his hand one night, on going to bed.

As I came downstairs next morning, shivering in the cold December air; colder in my uncle's unwarmed house than in the street, where the winter sun did sometimes shine, and which was at all events enlivened by cheerful faces and voices passing along; I carried a heavy heart towards the long, low breakfast-room in which my uncle sat. It was a large room with a small fire, and there was a great bay window in it which the rain had marked in the night as if with the tears of houseless people. It stared upon a raw yard, with a cracked stone pavement, and some rusted iron railings half uprooted, whence an ugly outbuilding that had once been a dissecting-room (in the time of the great surgeon who had mortgaged the house to my uncle), stared at it.

We rose so early always, that at that time of the year we breakfasted by candle-light. When I went into the room, my uncle was so contracted by the cold, and so huddled together in his chair behind the one dim candle, that I did not see him until I was close to the table.

As I held out my hand to him, he caught up his stick (being infirm, he always walked about the house with a stick), and made a blow at me, and said, 'You fool!'

'Uncle,' I returned, 'I didn't expect you to be so angry as this.' Nor had I expected it, though he was a hard and angry old man.

'You didn't expect!' said he; 'when did you ever expect? When did you ever calculate, or look forward, you contemptible dog?'

'These are hard words, uncle!'

'Hard words? Feathers, to pelt such an idiot as you with,' said he. 'Here! Betsy Snap! Look at him!'

Betsy Snap was a withered, hard-favoured, yellow old woman – our only domestic – always employed, at this time of the morning, in rubbing my uncle's legs. As my uncle adjured her to look at me, he put his lean grip on the crown of her head, she kneeling beside him, and turned her face towards me. An involuntary thought connecting them both with the Dissecting Room, as it must often have been in the surgeon's time, passed across my mind in the midst of my anxiety.

'Look at the snivelling milksop!' said my uncle. 'Look at the baby! This is the gentleman who, people say, is nobody's enemy but his own. This is the gentleman who can't say no. This is the gentleman who was making such large profits in his business that he must needs take a partner, t'other day. This is the gentleman who is going to marry a wife without a penny, and who falls into the hands of Jezebels who are speculating on my death!'

I knew, now, how great my uncle's rage was; for nothing short of his being almost beside himself would have induced him to utter that concluding word, which he held in such repugnance that it was never spoken or hinted at before him on any account.

'On my death,' he repeated, as if he were defying me by defying his own abhorrence of the word. 'On my death – death – Death! But I'll spoil the speculation. Eat your last under this roof, you feeble wretch, and may it choke you!'

You may suppose that I had not much appetite for the breakfast to which I was bidden in these terms; but, I took my accustomed seat. I saw that I was repudiated henceforth by my uncle; still I could bear that very well, possessing Christiana's heart.

He emptied his basin of bread and milk as usual, only that he took it on his knees with his chair turned away from the table where I sat. When he had done, he carefully snuffed out the candle; and the cold, slate-coloured, miserable day looked in upon us.

'Now, Mr. Michael,' said he, 'before we part, I should like to have a word with these ladies in your presence.'

'As you will, Sir,' I returned; 'but you deceive yourself, and wrong us, cruelly, if you suppose that there is any feeling at stake in this contract but pure, disinterested, faithful love.'

To this, he only replied, 'You lie!' and not one other word.

We went, through half-thawed snow and half-frozen rain, to the house where Christiana and her mother lived. My uncle knew them very well. They were sitting at their breakfast, and were surprised to see us at that hour.

'Your servant, ma'am,' said my uncle to the mother. 'You divine the purpose of my visit, I dare say, ma'am. I understand there is a world of pure, disinterested, faithful love cooped up here. I am happy to bring it all it wants, to make it complete. I bring you your son-in-law, ma'am – and you, your husband, miss. The gentleman is a perfect stranger to me, but I wish him joy of his wise bargain.'

He snarled at me as he went out, and I never saw him again.

It is altogether a mistake (continued the poor relation) to suppose that my dear Christians, over-persuaded and influenced by her mother, married a rich man, the dirt from whose carriage-wheels is often, in these changed times, thrown upon me as she rides by. No, no. She married me.

The way we came to be married rather sooner than we intended, was this. I took a frugal lodging and was saving and planning for her sake, when, one day, she spoke to me with great earnestness, and said:

'My dear Michael, I have given you my heart. I have said that I loved you, and I have pledged myself to be your wife. I am as much yours through all changes of good and evil as if we had been married on the day when such words passed between us. I know you well, and know that if we should be separated and our union broke off, your whole life would be shadowed, and all that might, even now, be stronger in your character for the conflict with the world would then be weakened to the shadow of what it is!'

'God help me, Christiana!' said I. 'You speak the truth.'

'Michael!' said she, putting her hand in mine, in all maidenly devotion, 'let us keep apart no longer. It is but for me to say that I can live contented upon such means as you have, and I well know you are happy. I say so from my heart. Strive no more alone; let us strive together. My dear Michael, it is not right that I should keep secret from you what you do not suspect, but what distresses my whole life. My mother: without considering that what you have lost, you have lost for me, and on the assurance of my faith: sets her heart on riches, and urges another suit upon me, to my misery. I cannot bear this, for to bear it is to be untrue to you. I would rather share your struggles than look on. I want no better home than you can give me. I know that you will aspire and labour with a higher courage if I am wholly yours, and let it be so when you will!'

I was blest indeed, that day, and a new world opened to me. We were married in a very little while, and I took my wife to our happy home. That was the beginning of the residence I have spoken of; the Castle we have ever since inhabited together, dates from that time. All our children have been born in it. Our first child – now married – was a little girl, whom we called Christiana. Her son is so like Little Frank, that I hardly know which is which.

* * *

The current impression as to my partner's dealings with me is also quite erroneous. He did not begin to treat me coldly, as a poor simpleton, when my uncle and I so fatally quarrelled; nor did he afterwards gradually possess himself of our business and edge me out. On the contrary, he behaved to me with the utmost good faith and honour.

Matters between us took this turn: – On the day of my separation from my uncle, and even before the arrival at our counting-house of my trunks (which he sent after me, *not* carriage paid), I went down to our room of business, on our little wharf, overlooking the river; and there I told John Spatter what had happened. John did not say, in reply, that rich old relatives were palpable facts, and that love and sentiment were moonshine and fiction. He addressed me thus:

'Michael,' said John, 'we were at school together, and I generally had the knack of getting on better than you, and making a higher reputation.'

'You had, John,' I returned.

'Although,' said John, 'I borrowed your books and lost them; borrowed your pocket-money, and never repaid it; got you to buy my damaged knives at a higher price than I had given for them new; and to own to the windows that I had broken.'

'All not worth mentioning, John Spatter,' said I, 'but certainly true.'

'When you were first established in this infant business, which promises to thrive so well,' pursued John, 'I came to you, in my search for almost any employment, and you made me your clerk.'

'Still not worth mentioning, my dear John Spatter,' said I; 'still, equally true.'

'And finding that I had a good head for business, and that I was really useful *to* the business, you did not like to retain me in that capacity, and thought it an act of justice soon to make me your partner.'

'Still less worth mentioning than any of those other little circumstances you have recalled, John Spatter,' said I; 'for I was, and am, sensible of your merits and my deficiencies.'

'Now, my good friend,' said John, drawing my arm through his, as he had had a habit of doing at school; while two vessels outside the windows of our counting-house – which were shaped like the stern windows of a ship – went lightly down the river with the tide, as John and I might then be sailing away in company, and in trust and confidence, on our voyage of life; 'let there, under these friendly circumstances, be a right understanding between us. You are too easy, Michael. You are nobody's enemy but your own. If I were to give you that damaging character among our connexion, with a shrug, and a shake of the head, and a sigh; and if I were further to abuse the trust you place in me – '

'But you never will abuse it at all, John,' I observed.

'Never!' said he: 'but I am putting a case – I say, and if I were further to abuse that trust by keeping this piece of our common affairs in the dark, and this other piece in the light, and again this other piece in the twilight, and so on, I should strengthen my strength, and weaken your weakness, day by day, until at last I found myself on the high road to fortune, and you left behind on some bare common, a hopeless number of miles out of the way.'

'Exactly so,' said I.

'To prevent this, Michael,' said John Spatter, 'or the remotest chance of this, there must be perfect openness between us. Nothing must be concealed, and we must have but one interest.'

'My dear John Spatter,' I assured him, 'that is precisely what I mean.'

'And when you are too easy,' pursued John, his face glowing with friendship, 'you must allow me to prevent that imperfection in your nature from being taken advantage of, by any one; you must not expect me to humour it – '

'My dear John Spatter,' I interrupted, 'I *don't* expect you to humour it. I want to correct it.'

'And I, too,' said John.

'Exactly so!' cried I. 'We both have the same end in view; and, honourably seeking it, and fully trusting one another, and having but one interest, ours will be a prosperous and happy partnership.'

'I am sure of it!' returned John Spatter. And we shook hands most affectionately.

I took John home to my Castle, and we had a very happy day. Our partnership throve well. My friend and partner supplied what I wanted, as I had foreseen that he would; and by improving both the business and myself, amply acknowledged any little rise in life to which I had helped him.

I am not (said the poor relation, looking at the fire as he slowly rubbed his hands) very rich, for I never cared to be that; but I have enough, and am above all moderate wants and anxieties. My Castle is not a splendid place, but it is very comfortable, and it has a warm and cheerful air, and is quite a picture of Home.

Our eldest girl, who is very like her mother, married John Spatter's eldest son. Our two families are closely united in other ties of attachment. It is very pleasant of an evening, when we are all assembled together – which frequently happens – and when John and I talk over old times, and the one interest there has always been between us.

I really do not know, in my Castle, what loneliness is. Some of our children or grandchildren are always about it, and the young voices of my descendants are delightful – O, how delightful! – to me to hear. My dearest and most devoted wife, ever faithful, ever loving, ever helpful and sustaining and consoling, is the priceless blessing of my house; from whom all its other blessings spring. We are rather a musical family, and when Christiana sees me, at any time, a little weary or depressed, she steals to the piano and sings a gentle air she used to sing when we were first betrothed. So weak a man am I, that I cannot bear to hear it from any other source. They played it once, at the Theatre, when I was there with Little Frank; and the child said wondering, 'Cousin Michael, whose hot tears are these that have fallen on my hand?'

Such is my Castle, and such are the real particulars of my life therein preserved. I often take Little Frank home there. He is very welcome to my grandchildren, and they play together. At this time of the year – the Christmas and New Year time – I am seldom out of my Castle. For, the associations of the season seem to hold me there, and the precepts of the season seem to teach me that it is well to be there.

'And the Castle is – ' observed a grave, kind voice among the company.

'Yes. My Castle,' said the poor relation, shaking his head as he still looked at the fire, 'is in the Air. John our esteemed host suggests its situation accurately. My Castle is in the Air! I have done. Will you be so good as to pass the story!'

Willa Cather 1873–1947

Willa Cather was born in Virginia, USA, into a farming family who moved to the mid-western state of Nebraska when she was nine years old. Her father's sheep farm had failed and he decided to join his father and brother, already lured to this prairie state by promises of rich farming land.

Once in Nebraska, Cather found herself amongst hardy, pioneering folk. As she recorded later – 'We had very few American neighbours, they were mainly Swedes, Dutch and Norwegian – I liked them from the first.' Few of the inhabitants of Red Cloud, Nebraska, spoke much English, but they managed to tell the young Willa a great many stories.

Cather's grandparents were deeply religious people for whom hellfire and eternal damnation were everyday realities. Most of her later writing was to draw on her experience of these early years.

When she was seventeen Cather enrolled at the University of Nebraska where she studied English for five years. It was here she started writing, and as editor of the college literary magazine, published a number of short stories dealing with the harsh realities of pioneer life.

Whilst still at college, Cather began her journalistic career, becoming a drama critic for the Nebraska State Journal. After graduating in 1896, she moved East, following an invitation to edit *Home Monthly* a magazine, based in Pittsburg. After a brief career break as a high school teacher, Cather moved again in 1904, this time to New York to edit the well established *McClures* magazine.

McClures had first published work from a number of writers admired by Cather, including Thomas Hardy, Arnold Bennett and Sir Arthur Conan Doyle. She then published her major novels, notably *O Pioneers* (1913) and the Pulitzer Prize winning *One of Ours* (1922). Cather was to continue a successful life writing literary journalism and fiction until her death in 1947 at the age of 72.

Lou, the Prophet (1892) was Cather's second published story; she was just nineteen years old. The story is a familiar mix of death and despair set within the Nebraska farming community. Lou, a simple, kindly and hard working young Dane has been trying to scratch a living from the reluctant prairie for seven long years. He is rewarded for his efforts by drought and crop failure. These disasters drive him to the very edge of sanity. He becomes a religious fanatic – endlessly fascinating to his small band of youthful followers but deeply disturbing to the rest of the community, who want to lock him away.

Lou, the Prophet

Willa Cather

It had been a very trying summer to every one, and most of all to Lou. He had been in the West for seven years, but he had never quite gotten over his homesickness for Denmark. Among the northern people who emigrate to the great west, only the children and the old people ever long much for the lands they have left over the water. The men only know that in this new land their plow runs across the field tearing up the fresh, warm earth, with never a stone to stay its course. That if they dig and delve the land long enough, and if they are not compelled to mortgage it to keep body and soul together, some day it will be theirs, their very own. They are not like the southern people; they lose their love for their fatherland quicker and have less of sentiment about them. They have to think too much about how they shall get bread to care much what soil gives it to them. But among even the most blunted, mechanical people, the youths and the aged always have a touch of romance in them.

Lou was only twenty-two; he had been but a boy when his family left Denmark, and had never ceased to remember it. He was a rather simple fellow, and was always considered less promising than his brothers; but last year he had taken up a claim of his own and made a rough dugout upon it and he lived there all alone. His life was that of many another young man in our country. He rose early in the morning, in the summer just before daybreak; in the winter, long before. First he fed his stock, then himself, which was a much less important matter. He ate the same food at dinner that he ate at breakfast, and the same at supper that he ate at dinner. His bill of fare never changed the year round; bread, coffee, beans and sorghum molasses, sometimes a little salt pork. After breakfast he worked until dinner time, ate, and then worked again. He always went to bed soon after the sunset, for he was always tired, and it saved oil. Sometimes, on Sundays, he would go over home after he had done his washing and house cleaning, and sometimes he hunted. His life was as sane and as uneventful as the life of his plow horses, and it was as hard and thankless. He was thrifty for a simple, thickheaded fellow, and in the spring he was to have married Nelse Sorenson's daughter, but he had lost all his cattle during the winter, and was not so prosperous as he had hoped to be; so, instead she married her cousin, who had an 'eighty' of his own. That hurt Lou more than anyone ever dreamed.

A few weeks later his mother died. He had always loved his mother. She had been kind to him and used to come over to see him sometimes, and shake up his hard bed for him, and sweep, and make his bread. She had a strong affection for the boy, he was her youngest, and she always felt sorry for him; she had danced a great deal before his birth, and an old woman in Denmark had told her that was the cause of the boy's weak head.

Perhaps the greatest calamity of all was the threatened loss of his corn crop. He had brought a new corn planter on time that spring, and had intended that his corn should pay for it. Now, it looked as though he would not have corn enough to feed his horses. Unless rain fell within the next two weeks, his entire crop would be ruined; it was half gone now. All these things together were too much for poor Lou, and one morning he felt a strange loathing for the bread and sorghum which he usually ate as mechanically as he slept. He kept thinking about the strawberries he used to gather on the mountains after the snows were gone, and the cold water in the mountain streams. He felt hot someway, and wanted cold water. He had no well, and he hauled his water from a neighbor's well every Sunday, and it got warm in the barrels those hot summer days. He worked at his haying all day; at night, when he was through feeding, he stood a long time by the pig stye with a basket on his arm. When the moon came up, he sighed restlessly and tore the buffalo pea flowers with his bare toes. After a while, he put his basket away, and went into his hot, close, little dugout. He did not sleep well, and he dreamed a horrible dream. He thought he saw the Devil and all his angels in the air holding back the rain clouds, and they loosed all the damned in Hell, and they came, poor tortured things, and drank up whole clouds of rain. Then he thought a strange light shone from the south, just over the river bluffs, and the clouds parted, and Christ and all his angels were descending. They were coming, coming, myriads and myriads of them, in a greater blaze of glory. Then he felt something give way in his poor, weak head, and with a cry of pain he awoke. He lay shuddering a long time in the dark, then got up and lit his lantern and took from the shelf his mother's Bible. It opened of itself at Revelation, and Lou began to read, slowly indeed, for it was hard work for him. Page by page, he read those burning, blinding, blasting words, and they seemed to shrivel from his hands and he sank down upon his knees in prayer, and stayed so until the dull gray dawn stole over the land and he heard the pigs clamoring for their feed.

He worked about the place until noon, and then prayed and read again. So he went on several days, praying and reading and fasting, until he grew thin and haggard. Nature did not comfort him any, he knew nothing about nature, he had never seen her; he had only stared into a black plow furrow all his life. Before, he had only seen in the wide, green lands and the open blue the possibilities of earning his bread; now, he only saw in them a great world ready for the judgement, a funeral pyre ready for the torch.

One morning, he went over to the big prairie dog town, where several little Danish boys herded their fathers' cattle. The boys were very fond of Lou; he never teased them as the other men did, but used to help them with their cattle, and let them come over to his dugout to make sorghum taffy.* When they saw him coming, they ran to meet him and asked him where he had been all these days. He did not answer their questions, but said: 'Come into the cave, I want to see you.'

* sweets

Some six or eight boys herded near the dog town every summer, and by their combined efforts they had dug a cave in the side of a high bank. It was large enough to hold them all comfortably, and high enough to stand in. There the boys used to go when it rained or when it was cold in the fall. They followed Lou silently and sat down on the floor. Lou stood up and looked tenderly down into the little faces before him. They were old-faced little fellows, though they were not over twelve or thirteen years old, hard work matures boys quickly.

'Boys,' he said earnestly, 'I have found out why it don't rain, it's because of the sins of the world. You don't know how wicked the world is, it's all bad, all, even Denmark. People have been sinning a long time, but they won't much longer. God has been watching and watching for thousands of years, and filling up the phials of wrath, and now he is going to pour out his vengeance and let Hell loose upon the world. He is burning up our corn now, and worse things will happen; for the sun shall be as sackcloth, and the moon shall be like blood, and the stars of heaven shall fall, and the heavens shall part like a scroll, and the mountains shall be moved out of their places, and the great day of his wrath shall come, against which none may stand. Oh, boys! the floods and flames shall come down upon us together and the whole world shall perish.' Lou paused for breath, and the little boys gazed at him in wonder. The sweat was running down his haggard face, and his eyes were staring wildly. Presently, he resumed in a softer tone, 'Boys, if you want rain, there is only one way to get it, by prayer. The people of the world won't pray, perhaps if they did God would not hear them, for they are so wicked; but he will hear you, for you are little children and are likened unto the kingdom of heaven, and he loved ye.'

Lou's haggard, unshaven face bent toward them and his blue eyes gazed at them with terrible earnestness.

'Show us how, Lou,' said one little fellow in an awed whisper. Lou knelt down in the cave, his long, shaggy hair hung down over his face, and his voice trembled as he spoke:

'Oh God, they call thee many long names in thy book,

thy prophets; but we are only simple folk, the boys are all little and I am weak headed ever since I was born, therefore, let us call thee Father, for thy other names are hard to remember. O Father, we are so thirsty, all the world is thirsty; the creeks are all dried up, and the river is so low that the fishes die and rot in it; the corn is almost gone; the hay is light; and even the little flowers are no more beautiful. Oh God! our corn may yet be saved. O, give us rain! Our corn means so much to us, if it fails, all our pigs and cattle will die, and we ourselves come very near to it; but if you do not send rain, O Father, and if the end is indeed come, be merciful to thy great, wicked world. They do many wrong things, but I think they forget thy word, for it is a long book to remember, and some are little and some are born weak headed, like me, and some are born very strong headed, which is near as bad. Oh, forgive them their abominations in all the world, both in Denmark and here, for the fire hurts so, O God! Amen.'

The little boys knelt and each said a few blundering words. Outside, the sun shone brightly and the cattle nibbled at the short, dry grass, and the hot wind blew through the shriveled corn; within the cave, they knelt as many another had knelt before them, some in temples, some in prison cells, some in the caves of earth, and One, indeed, in the garden, praying for the sin of the world.

The next day, Lou went to town, and prayed in the streets. When the people saw his emaciated frame and wild eyes, and heard his wild words, they told the sheriff to do his duty, the man must be mad. Then Lou ran away; he ran for miles, then walked and limped and stumbled on, until he reached the cave; there the boys found him in the morning. The officials hunted him for days, but he hid in the cave, and the little Danes kept his secret well. They shared their dinners with him, but now they would have gone straight through fire for him, any one of them, they almost worshipped him. He had about him that mysticism which always appeals so quickly to children. I have always thought that bear story which the Hebrews used to tell their children very improbable. If it was true, then I have my doubts about the prophet; no one in the world will hoot at insincere and affected piety sooner than a child, but no one feels the true prophetic flame quicker, no one is more readily touched by simple goodness. A very young child can tell a sincere man better than any phrenologist.

One morning, he told the boys that he had had another 'true dream.' He was not going to die like other men, but God was going to take him to himself as he was. The end of the world was close at hand, too very close. He prayed more than usual that day, and when they sat eating their dinner in the sunshine, he suddenly sprang to his feet and stared wildly south, crying. 'See, see, it is the great light! the end comes!! and they do not know it; they will keep on sinning. I must tell them, I must!'

'No, no, Lou, they will catch you; they are looking for you, you must not go!'

'I must go, my boys; but first let me speak once more to you. Men would not heed me, or believe me, because my head is weak, but you have always believed in me, that God has revealed his word to me, and I will pray God to take you to himself quickly, for ye are worthy. Watch and pray always, boys, watch the light over the bluffs, it is breaking, breaking, and shall grow brighter. Goodbye, my boys, I must leave ye in the world yet awhile.' He kissed them all tenderly and blessed them, and started south. He walked at first, then he ran, faster and faster he went, all the while shouting at the top of his voice, 'The sword of the Lord and of Gideon!'

The police officers heard of it, and set out to find him. They hunted the country over and even dragged the river, but they never found him again, living or dead. It is thought that he was drowned and the quicksands of the river sucked his body under. But the little Dane boys in our country firmly believed that he was translated like Enoch of old. On stormy nights, when the great winds sweep down from the north they huddle together in their beds and fancy that in the wind they still hear that wild cry, 'The sword of the Lord and of Gideon.'

H. G. Wells 1866–1946

Herbert George Wells is best known as the author of fantasy and science fiction novels: *The Time Machine (1895), The Invisible Man* (1897) and *The War of the Worlds* (1898). These novels, written at the end of the nineteenth century at a time of rapid social and industrial change, explore ideas about what the world of the twentieth century and beyond might be like.

Wells' own early experiences made him want to question much about the Victorian age he grew up in. He was born in 1866 in Bromley, Kent, the youngest of three sons. His father, Joseph, earned a meagre living running a general shop and playing professional cricket. When Joseph Wells broke his leg and could no longer earn a living, 13-year-old Herbert was sent to work in a draper's shop. His mother became a housekeeper in a grand country house and on his visits there Herbert would secretly study the books in the library. He finally managed to win a scholarship to study science at what is now Imperial College, London. Wells was concerned about social justice and joined a socialist movement, The Fabian Society. This group of intellectuals sought to bring about a fairer society by planning for a gradual system of reforms.

Wells' interest in science and politics combine in this story, *The Stolen Bacillus* (1894). There are many touches which make it seem relevant today – the research scientist working to understand and control a dangerous disease; the dangerous anarchist visitor who seeks to make his mark on the world with his own brand of germ warfare; the deadly disease which 'might multiply and devastate a city'. Even the chase, which involves three horse-drawn cabs, reads rather like the script from a contemporary film.

You may feel rather less comfortable with other aspects of the story – for example the dutiful wife Minnie who chases after her husband with his hat, coat and shoes or the cabmen who emerge as comic caricatures with their exaggerated, 'common' speech. The ending holds its own surprise and no doubt you will want to consider how well it works for you.

The Stolen Bacillus

H. G. Wells

'This again,' said the Bacteriologist,* slipping a glass slide under the miscroscope, 'is a preparation of the celebrated Bacillus of cholera – the cholera germ.'

The pale-faced man peered down the microscope. He was evidently not accustomed to that kind of thing, and held a limp white hand over his disengaged eye. 'I see very little,' he said.

'Touch this screw,' said the Bacteriologist; 'perhaps the microscope is out of focus for you. Eyes vary so much. Just the fraction of a turn this way or that.'

'Ah! now I see,' said the visitor. 'Not so very much to see after all. Little streaks and shreds of pink. And yet those little particles, those mere atomies, might multiply and devastate a city! Wonderful!'

He stood up, and releasing the glass slip from the microscope, held it in his hand towards the window. 'Scarcely visible,' he said, scrutinizing the preparation. He hesitated, 'Are these – alive? Are they dangerous now?'

'Those have been stained and killed,' said the Bacteriologist. 'I wish, for my own part, we could kill and stain every one of them in the universe.'

'I suppose,' the pale man said with a slight smile, 'that you scarcely care to have such things about you in the living – in the active state?'

'On the contrary, we are obliged to,' said the Bacteriologist. 'Here, for instance – ' He walked across the room and took up one of several sealed tubes. 'Here is the living

* a scientist who studies bacteria.
a bacillus is a single bacterium.

thing. This is a cultivation of the actual living disease bacteria.' He hesitated. 'Bottled cholera, so to speak.'

A slight gleam of satisfaction appeared momentarily in the face of the pale man. 'It's a deadly thing to have in your possession,' he said, devouring the little tube with his eyes. The Bacteriologist watched the morbid pleasure in his visitor's expression. This man, who had visited him that afternoon with a note of introduction from an old friend, interested him from the very contrast of their dispositions. The lank black hair and deep grey eyes, the haggard expression and nervous manner, the fitful yet keen interest in his visitor, were a novel change from the phlegmatic deliberations of the ordinary scientific worker with whom the Bacteriologist chiefly associated. It was perhaps natural, with a hearer evidently so impressionable to the lethal nature of his topic, to take the most effective aspect of the matter.

He held the tube in his hand thoughtfully. 'Yes, here is the pestilence imprisoned. Only break such a little tube as this into a supply of drinking-water, say to these minute particles of life that one must needs stain and examine with the highest powers of the microscope even to see, and that one can neither smell nor taste – say to them, "Go forth, increase and multiply, and replenish the cisterns", and death – mysterious, untraceable death, death swift and terrible, death full of pain and indignity – would be released upon this city, and go hither and thither seeking his victims. Here he would take the husband from the wife, here the child from its mother, here the statesman from his duty, and here the toiler from his trouble. He would follow the water-mains, creeping along streets, picking out and punishing a house here and a house there where they did not boil their drinking-water, creeping into the wells of the mineral-water makers, getting washed into salad, and lying dormant in ices. He would wait ready to be drunk in the horse-troughs, and by unwary children in the public fountains. He would soak into the soil, to reappear in springs and wells at a thousand unexpected places. Once start him at the water supply, and before we could ring him in, and catch him again, he would have decimated the metropolis.'

He stopped abuptly. He had been told rhetoric was his weakness.

'But he is quite safe here, you know – quite safe.'

The pale-faced man nodded. His eyes shone. He cleared his throat. 'These Anarchist – rascals,' said he, 'are fools, blind fools – to use bombs when this kind of thing is attainable. I think – '

A gentle rap, a mere light touch of the finger-nails was heard at the door. The Bacteriologist opened it. 'Just a minute, dear,' whispered his wife.

When he re-entered the laboratory his visitor was looking at his watch. 'I had no idea I had wasted an hour of your time,' he said. 'Twelve minutes to four. I ought to have left here by half past three. But your things were really too interesting. No, positively I cannot stop a moment longer. I have an engagement at four.'

He passed out of the room, reiterating his thanks, and the Bacteriologist accompanied him to the door, and then returned thoughtfully along the passage to his laboratory. He was musing on the ethnology* of his visitor. Certainly the man was not a Teutonic type nor a common Latin one. 'A morbid product, anyhow, I am afraid,' said the Bacteriologist to himself. 'How he gloated on those cultivations of disease-germs!' A disturbing thought struck him. He turned to the bench by the vapour-bath, and then very quickly to his writing-table. Then he felt hastily in his pockets, and then rushed to the door. 'I may have put it down on the hall table,' he said.

'Minnie!' he shouted hoarsely in the hall.

'Yes, dear,' came a remote voice.

'Had I anything in my hand when I spoke to you, dear, just now?'

Pause.

'Nothing, dear, because I remember – '

'Blue ruin!' cried the Bacteriologist, and incontinently† ran to the front door and down the steps of his house to the street.

Minnie, hearing the door slam violently, ran in alarm to the window. Down the street a slender man was getting

* ethnic background † immediately

into a cab. The Bacteriologist, hatless, and in his carpet slippers, was running and gesticulating wildly towards this group. One slipper came off, but he did not wait for it. 'He has gone *mad*!' said Minnie; 'it's that horrid science of his'; and, opening the window, would have called after him. The slender man, suddenly glancing round, seemed struck with the same idea of mental disorder. He pointed hastily to the Bacteriologist, said something to the cabman, the apron of the cab slammed, the whip swished, the horse's feet clattered, and in a moment the cab, Bacteriologist hotly in pursuit, had receded up the vista of the roadway and disappeared round the corner.

Minnie remained straining out of the window for a minute. Then she drew her head back into the room again. She was dumbfounded. 'Of course he is eccentric,' she meditated. 'But running about London – in the height of the season, too – in his socks!' A happy thought struck her. She hastily put her bonnet on, seized his shoes, went into the hall, took down his hat and light overcoat from the pegs, emerged upon the doorstep, and hailed a cab that opportunely crawled by. 'Drive me up the road and round Havelock Crescent, and see if we can find a gentleman running about in a velveteen coat and no hat.'

'Velveteen coat, ma'am and no 'at. Very good, ma'am.' And the cabman whipped up at once in the most matter-of-fact way, as if he drove to this address every day in his life.

Some few minutes later the little group of cabmen and loafers that collects round the cabmen's shelter at Haverstock Hill were startled by the passing of a cab with a ginger-coloured screw of a horse, driven furiously.

They were silent as it went by, and then as it receded – 'That's 'Arry 'Icks. Wot's *he* got?' said the stout gentleman known as Old Tootles.

'He's a-using his whip, he is, *to* rights,' said the ostler boy.

'Hullo!' said poor old Tommy Byles; 'here's another bloomin' loonatic. Blowed if there ain't.'

'It's old George,' said Old Tootles, 'and he's drivin' a loonatic, *as* you say. Ain't he a-clawin' out of the keb? Wonder if he's after 'Arry 'Icks?'

The group round the cabmen's shelter became animated. Chorus: 'Go it, George!' 'It's a race!' 'You'll ketch 'em!' 'Whip up!'

'She's a goer, she is!' said the ostler boy.

'Strike me giddy!' cried Old Tootles. 'Here! *I'm* a-goin' to begin in a minute. Here's another comin'. If all the kebs in Hampstead ain't gone mad this morning!'

'It's a female this time,' said the ostler boy.

'She's a-following *him*,' said Old Tootles. 'Usually the other way about.'

'What's she got in her 'and?'

'Looks like a 'igh 'at.'

'What a bloomin' lark it is! Three to one on old George,' said the ostler boy. 'Next!'

Minnie went by in a perfect roar of applause. She did not like it but she felt that she was doing her duty, and whirled on down Haverstock Hill and Camden Town High Street with her eyes ever intent on the animated back of Old George, who was driving her vagrant husband so incomprehensively away from her.

The man in the foremost cab sat crouched in the corner, his arms tightly folded, and the little tube that contained such vast possibilities of destruction gripped in his hand. His mood was a singular mixture of fear and exultation. Chiefly he was afraid of being caught before he could accomplish his purpose, but behind this was a vaguer but larger fear of the awfulness of his crime. But his exultation far exceeded his fear. No Anarchist before him had ever approached this conception of his. Ravachol, Vaillant, all those distinguished persons whose fame he had envied, dwindled into insignificance beside him. He had only to make sure of the water supply, and break the little tube into a reservoir. How brilliantly he had planned it, forged the letter of introduction, and got into the laboratory, and how brilliantly he had seized his opportunity! The world should hear of him at last. All those people who had sneered at him, neglected him, preferred other people to him, found his company undesirable, should consider him at last. Death, death, death! They had always treated him as a man of no importance. All the world had been in a conspiracy to keep him under. He would teach them yet what it is to isolate a man. What was this familiar street? Great Saint Andrew's Street, of course! How fared the chase? He craned out of the cab. The Bacteriologist was scarcely fifty yards behind. That was bad. He would be caught and stopped yet. He felt in his pocket for money, and found half a sovereign. This he thrust up through the trap in the top of the cab into the man's face. 'More,' he shouted, 'if only we get away.'

The money was snatched out of his hand. 'Right you are,' said the cabman, and the trap slammed, and the lash lay along the glistening side of the horse. The cab swayed, and the Anarchist, half-standing under the trap, put the hand containing the little glass tube upon the apron to preserve his balance. He felt the brittle thing crack, and the broken half of it rang upon the floor of the cab. He fell back into the seat with a curse, and stared dismally at the two or three drops of moisture on the apron.

He shuddered.

'Well! I suppose I shall be the first. *Phew!* Anyhow, I shall be a Martyr. That's something. But it is a filthy death, nevertheless. I wonder if it hurts as much as they say.'

Presently a thought occurred to him – he groped between his feet. A little drop was still in the broken end of the tube, and he drank that to make sure. It was better to make sure. At any rate, he would not fail.

Then it dawned upon him that there was no further need to escape the Bacteriologist. In Wellington Street he told the cabman to stop and got out. He slipped on the step, his head felt queer. It was rapid stuff this cholera poison. He waved his cabman out of existence, so to speak, and stood on the pavement with his arm folded upon his breast, awaiting the arrival of the Bacteriologist. There was something tragic in his pose. The sense of imminent death gave him a certain dignity. He greeted his pursuer with a defiant laugh.

'*Vive l'Anarchie!* You are too late, my friend. I have drunk it. The cholera is abroad!'

The Bacteriologist from his cab beamed curiously at him through his spectacles. 'You have drunk it! An Anarchist! I see now.' He was about to say something more, and then checked himself. A smile hung in the corner of his mouth. He opened the apron of his cab as if to descend, at which the Anarchist waved him a dramatic farewell and strode off towards Waterloo Bridge, carefully jostling his infected body against as many people as possible. The Bacteriologist was so preoccupied with the vision of him that he scarcely manifested the slightest surprise at the appearance of Minnie upon the pavement with his hat and shoes and overcoat. 'Very good of you to bring my things,' he said, and remained lost in contemplation of the receding figure of the Anarchist.

'You had better get in,' he said, still staring. Minnie felt absolutely convinced now that he was mad, and directed the cabman home on her own responsibility. 'Put on my shoes? Certainly, dear,' said he, as the cab began to turn, and hid the strutting black figure, now small in the distance, from his eyes. Then suddenly something grotesque struck him, and he laughed. Then he remarked, 'It is really very serious, though.

'You see, that man came to my house to see me, and he is an Anarchist. No – don't faint, or I cannot possibly tell you the rest. And I wanted to astonish him, not knowing he was an Anarchist, and took up a cultivation of that new species of Bacterium I was telling you of, that infest, and I think cause, the blue patches upon various monkeys; and like a fool, I said it was Asiatic cholera. And he ran away with it to poison the water of London, and he certainly might have made things look blue for this civilized city. And now he has swallowed it. Of course, I cannot say what will happen, but you know it turned that kitten blue, and the three puppies – in patches, and the sparrow – bright blue. But the bother is, I shall have all the trouble and expense of preparing some more.

'Put on my coat on this hot day! Why? Because we might meet Mrs Jabber. My dear, Mrs Jabber is not a draught. But why should I wear a coat on a hot day because of Mrs —? Oh! *very* well.'

Edgar Allan Poe 1809–1849

Author of *The Tell Tale Heart* and *The Pit and the Pendulum*, Edgar Allan Poe is possibly the best known American writer of the nineteenth century. Although most of his writing can be found under such headings as 'Horror' or 'The Supernatural', he, in fact, wrote widely in many areas including, in *The Purloined Letter*, the first ever detective story.

Born in Boston to a theatrical family, Poe's mother died when he was two years old. Edgar was taken in and thereafter raised by the Allan family – hence Edgar Allan Poe. This unsettled childhood continued into his teens and after a brief spell at the University of Virginia, he was expelled for drunkeness and debt. Although he had no obvious interest in military matters, Poe joined the Army, and was fortunate in being offered a teaching post at the prestigious West Point military academy. However, his unruly private life again got the better of him when he was court martialled in 1831 for gambling and drunkeness; his teaching post was taken from him.

From this time on Poe was under considerable financial pressure. This was probably the spur for him to begin writing for a living. Poe immersed himself in the world of literary magazines, contributing to many, covering a range of topics and a variety of styles. The shadow of scandal remained however, and in 1836 he married Virginia, the thirteen-year-old daughter of his favourite aunt. Virginia died in suspicious circumstances eleven years later and a series of semi-public love affairs followed. *Hop-Frog* was one of his last stories to be published before his own early death in 1849.

Hop-Frog, written in 1849, is a typically strange story of a tyrant king with a taste for weird practical jokes and a court jester, determined to seek revenge on his cruel master. Not a comforting read, *Hop-Frog* challenges accepted ideas about the powers of corruption and recrimination – it also happens to be Stephen King's favourite Edgar Allan Poe short story.

Hop-Frog
or
The Eight Chained Ourang-Outangs

Edgar Allan Poe

I never knew any one so keenly alive to a joke as the king was. He seemed to live only for joking. To tell a good story of the joke kind, and to tell it well, was the surest road to his favor. Thus it happened that his seven ministers were all noted for their accomplishments as jokers. They all took after the king, too, in being large, corpulent, oily men, as well as inimitable jokers. Whether people grow fat by joking, or whether there is something in fat itself which predisposes to a joke, I have never been quite able to determine; but certain it is that a lean joker is a *rara avis in terris*.*

About the refinements, or, as he called them, the 'ghosts' of wit, the king troubled himself very little. He had an especial admiration for *breadth* in a jest, and would often put up with *length*, for the sake of it. Over-niceties wearied him. He would have preferred Rabelais's 'Gargantua,' to the 'Zadig' of Voltaire:† and, upon the whole, practical jokes suited his taste far better than verbal ones.

At the date of my narrative, professing jesters had not altogether gone out of fashion at court. Several of the great continental 'powers' still retained their 'fools,' who wore motley, with caps and bells, and who were expected to be always ready with sharp witticisms, at a moment's notice, in consideration of the crumbs that fell from the royal table.

Our king, as a matter of course, retained his 'fool.' The fact is, he *required* something in the way of folly – if only

* a rare bird on this earth
† he preferred outrageousness to subtlety

to counterbalance the heavy wisdom of the seven wise men who were his ministers – not to mention himself.

His fool, or professional jester, was not *only* a fool, however. His value was trebled in the eyes of the king, by the fact of his being also a dwarf and a cripple. Dwarfs were as common at court, in those days, as fools; and many monarchs would have found it difficult to get through their days (days are rather longer at court than elsewhere) without both a jester to laugh *with*, and a dwarf to laugh *at*. But, as I have already observed, your jesters, in ninety-nine cases out of a hundred, are fat, round and unwieldly – so that it was no small source of self-gratification with our king that, in Hop-Frog (this was the fool's name), he possessed a triplicate treasure in one person.

I believe the name 'Hop-Frog' was *not* given to the dwarf by his sponsors at baptism, but it was conferred upon him, by general consent of the seven ministers, on account of his inability to walk as other men do. In fact, Hop-Frog could only get along by a sort of interjectional gait – something between a leap and a wriggle – a movement that afforded illimitable amusement, and of course consolation, to the king, for (notwithstanding the protuberance of his stomach and a constitutional swelling of the head) the king, by his whole court, was accounted a capital figure.

But although Hop-Frog, through the distortion of his legs, could move only with great pain and difficulty along a road or floor, the prodigious muscular power which nature seemed to have bestowed upon his arms, by way of compensation for deficiency in the lower limbs, enabled him to perform many feats of wonderful dexterity, where trees or ropes were in question, or anything else to climb. At such exercises he certainly much more resembled a squirrel, or a small monkey, than a frog.

I am not able to say, with precision, from what country Hop-Frog originally came. It was from some barbarous region, however, that no person ever heard of – a vast distance from the court of our king. Hop-Frog, and a young girl very little less dwarfish than himself (although of exquisite proportions, and a marvellous dancer), had been forcibly carried off from their respective homes in adjoining provinces, and sent as presents to the king, by one of his ever-victorious generals.

Under these circumstances, it is not to be wondered at that a close intimacy arose between the two little captives. Indeed, they soon became sworn friends. Hop-Frog, who, although he made a great deal of sport, was by no means popular, had it not in his power to render Trippetta many services; but *she*, on account of her grace and exquisite beauty (although a dwarf), was universally admired and petted: so she possessed much influence; and never failed to use it, whenever she could, for the benefit of Hop-Frog.

On some grand state occasion – I forget what – the king determined to have a masquerade; and whenever a masquerade, or anything of that kind, occurred at our court, then the talents both of Hop-Frog and Trippetta were sure to be called in play. Hop-Frog, in especial, was so inventive in the way of getting up pageants, suggesting novel characters, and arranging costume, for masked balls, that nothing could be done, it seems, without his assistance.

The night appointed for the *fête* had arrived. A gorgeous hall had been fitted up, under Trippetta's eye, with every kind of device which could possibly give *éclat** to a masquerade. The whole court was in a fever of expectation. As for costumes and characters, it might well be supposed that everybody had come to a decision on such points. Many had made up their minds (as to what *rôles* they should assume) a week, or even a month, in advance; and, in fact, there was not a particle of indecision anywhere – except in the case of the king and his seven ministers. Why *they* hesitated I never could tell, unless they did it by way of a joke. More probably, they found it difficult, on account of being so fat, to make up their minds. At all events, time flew; and, as a last resource, they sent for Trippetta and Hop-Frog.

When the two little friends obeyed the summons of the king, they found him sitting at his wine with the seven members of his cabinet council; but the monarch appeared to be in a very ill humor. He knew that Hop-Frog was not fond of wine; for it excited the poor cripple almost to

* make a showy display

madness; and madness is no comfortable feeling. But the king loved his practical jokes, and took pleasure in forcing Hop-Frog to drink and (as the king called it) 'to be merry.'

'Come here, Hop-Frog,' said he, as the jester and his friend entered the room: 'swallow this bumper to the health of your absent friends [here Hop-Frog sighed,] and then let us have the benefit of your invention. We want characters – *characters*, man – something novel – out of the way. We are wearied with this everlasting sameness. Come drink! the wine will brighten your wits.'

Hop-Frog endeavoured, as usual, to get up a jest in reply to these advances from the king; but the effort was too much. It happened to be the poor dwarf's birthday, and the command to drink to his 'absent friends' forced the tears to his eyes. Many large, bitter drops fell into the goblet as he took it, humbly, from the hand of the tyrant.

'Ah! ha! ha! ha!' roared the latter, as the dwarf reluctantly drained the beaker. 'See what a glass of good wine can do! Why, your eyes are shining already!'

Poor fellow, his large eyes *gleamed*, rather than shone; for the effect of wine on his excitable brain was not more powerful than instantaneous. He placed the goblet nervously on the table, and looked round upon the company with a half-insane stare. They all seemed highly amused at the success of the king's '*joke*.'

'And now to business,' said the prime minister, a *very* fat man.

'Yes,' said the king; 'come, Hop-Frog, lend us your assistance. Characters, my fine fellow; we stand in need of characters – all of us – ha! ha! ha!' and as this was seriously meant for a joke, his laugh was chorused by the seven.

Hop-Frog also laughed, although feebly and somewhat vacantly.

'Come, come,' said the king, impatiently, 'have you nothing to suggest?'

'I am endeavouring to think of something *novel*,' replied the dwarf, abstractedly, for he was quite bewildered by the wine.

'Endeavouring!' cried the tyrant, fiercely; 'what do you mean by *that*? Ah, I perceive. You are sulky, and want more wine. Here, drink this!' and he poured out another goblet full and offered it to the cripple, who merely gazed at it, gasping for breath.

'Drink, I say!' shouted the monster, 'or by the fiends – '

The dwarf hesitated. The king grew purple with rage. The courtiers smirked. Trippetta, pale as a corpse, advanced to the monarch's seat, and, falling on her knees before him, implored him to spare her friend.

The tyrant regarded her, for some moments, in evident wonder at her audacity. He seemed quite at a loss what to do or say – how most becomingly to express his indignation. At last, without uttering a syllable, he pushed her violently from him, and threw the contents of the brimming goblet in her face.

The poor girl got up as best she could, and, not daring even to sigh, resumed her position at the foot of the table.

There was a dead silence for about a half a minute, during which the falling of a leaf, or of a feather might have been heard. It was interrupted by a low, but harsh and protracted *grating* sound which seemed to come at once from every corner of the room.

'What – what – *what* are you making that noise for?' demanded the king, turning furiously to the dwarf.

The latter seemed to have recovered, in great measure from his intoxication, and looking fixedly but quietly into the tyrant's face, merely ejaculated:

'I – I? How could it have been me?'

'The sound appeared to come from without,' observed one of the courtiers. 'I fancy it was the parrot at the window, whetting his bill upon his cage-wires.'

'True,' replied the monarch, as if much relieved by the suggestion; 'but, on the honour of a knight, I could have sworn that it was the gritting of this vagabond's teeth.'

Hereupon the dwarf laughed (the king was too confirmed a joker to object to any one's laughing), and displayed a set of large, powerful, and very repulsive teeth. Moreover, he avowed his perfect willingness to swallow as much wine as desired. The monarch was pacified; and having drained another bumper with no very perceptible ill effect, Hop-Frog entered at once, and with spirit, into the plans for the masquerade.

'I cannot tell what was the association of idea,' observed

he, very tranquilly, and as if he had never tasted wine in his life, 'but *just after* your majesty had struck the girl and thrown the wine in her face – *just after* your majesty had done this, and while the parrot was making that odd noise outside the window, there came into my mind a capital diversion – one of my own country frolics – often enacted among us, at our masquerades: but here it will be new altogether. Unfortunately, however, it requires a company of eight persons, and – '

'Here we *are!*' cried the king, laughing at his acute discovery of the coincidence; 'eight to a fraction – I and my seven ministers. Come! what is the diversion?'

'We call it,' replied the cripple, 'the Eight Chained Ourang-Outangs, and it really is excellent sport if well enacted.'

'*We* will enact it,' remarked the king, drawing himself up, and lowering his eye-lids.

'The beauty of the game,' continued Hop-Frog, 'lies in the fright it occasions among the women.'

'Capital!' roared in chorus the monarch and his ministry.

'*I* will equip you as ourang-outangs,' proceeded the dwarf; 'leave all that to me. The resemblance shall be so striking, that the company of masqueraders will take you for real beasts – and, of course, they will be as much terrified as astonished.'

'O, this is exquisite!' exclaimed the king. 'Hop-Frog! I will make a man of you.'

'The chains are for the purpose of increasing the confusion by their jangling. You are supposed to have escaped, *en masse*, from your keepers. Your majesty cannot conceive the *effect* produced at a masquerade, by eight chained ourang-outangs, imagined to be real ones by most of the company; and rushing in with savage cries, among the crowd of delicately and gorgeously habited men and women. The *contrast* is inimitable.'

'It *must* be,' said the king: and the council arose hurriedly (as it was growing late), to put in execution the scheme of Hop-Frog.

His mode of equipping the party as ourang-outangs was very simple, but effective enough for his purposes. The animals in question had, at the epoch of my story, very rarely been seen in any part of the civilised world; and as the imitations made by the dwarf were sufficiently beast-like and more than sufficiently hideous, their truthfulness to nature was thus thought to be secured.

The king and his ministers were first encased in tight-fitting stockinet shirts and drawers. They were then saturated with tar. At this stage of the process, some one of the party suggested feathers; but the suggestion was at once overruled by the dwarf, who soon convinced the eight, by ocular demonstration, that the hair of such a brute as the ourang-outang was much more efficiently represented by *flax*. A thick coating of the latter was accordingly plastered upon the coating of tar. A long chain was now procured. First, it was passed about the waist of the king, *and tied*; then about another of the party, and also tied; then about all successively, in the same manner. When this chaining arrangement was complete, and the party stood as far apart from each other as possible, they formed a circle; and to make all things appear natural, Hop-Frog passed the residue of the chain, in two diameters, at right angles, across the circle, after the fashion adopted, at the present day, by those who capture Chimpanzees, or other large apes, in Borneo.

The grand saloon in which the masquerade was to take place, was a circular room, very lofty, and receiving the light of the sun only through a single window at top. At night (the season for which the apartment was especially designed), it was illuminated principally by a large chandelier, depending by a chain from the centre of the sky-light, and lowered, or elevated, by means of a counter-balance as usual; but (in order not to look unsightly) this latter passed outside the cupola and over the roof.

The arrangements of the room had been left to Trippetta's superintendance; but, in some particulars, it seems, she had been guided by the calmer judgement of her friend the dwarf. At his suggestion it was that, on this occasion, the chandelier was removed. Its waxen drippings (which, in weather so warm, it was quite impossible to prevent), would have been seriously detrimental to the rich dresses of the guests, who, on account of the crowded state of the saloon, could not *all* be expected to keep from out its centre

– that is to say, from under the chandelier. Additional sconces* were set in various parts of the hall, out of the way; and a flambeau,† emitting sweet odor, was placed in the right hand of each of the Caryatides‡ that stood against the wall – some fifty or sixty altogether.

The eight ourang-outangs, taking Hop-Frog's advice, waited patiently until midnight (when the room was thoroughly filled with masqueraders) before making their appearance. No sooner had the clock ceased striking, however, than they rushed, or rather rolled in, all together – for the impediment of their chains caused most of the party to fall, and all to stumble as they entered.

The excitement among the masqueraders was prodigious, and filled the heart of the king with glee. As had been anticipated, there were not a few of the guests who supposed the ferocious-looking creatures to be beasts of *some* kind in reality, if not precisely ourang-outangs. Many of the women swooned with affright; and had not the king taken precaution to exclude all weapons from the saloon, his party might soon have expiated their frolic in their blood. As it was, a general rush was made of the doors; but the king had ordered them to be locked immediately upon his entrance; and, at the dwarf's suggestion, the keys had been deposited with *him*.

While the tumult was at its height, and each masquerader attentive only to his own safety – (for, in fact, there was much *real* danger from the pressure of the excited crowd) – the chain by which the chandelier ordinarily hung, and which had been drawn up on its removal, might have been seen very gradually to descend, until its hooked extremity came within three feet of the floor.

Soon after this, the king and his seven friends, having reeled about the hall in all directions, found themselves, at length, in its centre, and, of course, in immediate contact with the chain. While they were thus situated, the dwarf, who had followed closely at their heels, inciting them to keep up the commotion, took hold of their own chain at the intersection of the two portions which crossed the circle diametrically and at right angles. Here, with the rapidity

* candlesticks † burning torch ‡ statue of Greek woman

of thought, he inserted the hook from which the chandelier had been wont to depend; and, in an instant, by some unseen agency, the chandelier-chain was drawn so far upward as to take the hook out of reach, and, as an inevitable consequence, to drag the ourang-outangs together in close connection, and face to face.

The masqueraders, by this time, had recovered, in some measure, from their alarm; and beginning to regard the whole matter as a well-contrived pleasantry, set up a loud shout of laughter at the predicament of the apes.

'Leave them to *me!*' now screamed Hop-Frog, his shrill voice making itself easily heard through all the din. 'Leave them to *me*. I fancy *I* know them. If I can only get a good look at them, *I* can soon tell who they are.'

Here, scrambling over the heads of the crowd, he managed to get to the wall, when, seizing a flambeau from one of the Caryatides, he returned, as he went, to the centre of the room – leaped, with the agility of a monkey, upon the king's head – and thence clambered a few feet up the chain – holding down the torch to examine the group of ourang-outangs, and still screaming. '*I* shall find out who they are!'

And now, while the whole assembly (the apes included!) were convulsed with laughter, the jester suddenly uttered a shrill whistle; when the chain flew violently up for about thirty feet – dragging with it the dismayed and struggling ourang-outangs, and leaving them suspended in mid-air between the sky-light and the floor. Hop-Frog, clinging to the chain as it rose, still maintained his relative position in respect to the eight maskers, and still (as if nothing were the matter) continued to thrust his torch down towards them, as though endeavoring to discover who they were.

So thoroughly astonished were the whole company at this ascent, that a dead silence, of about a minute's duration, ensued. It was broken by just such a low, harsh, *grating* sound, as had before attracted the attention of the king and his councillors, when the former threw the wine in the face of Trippetta. But, on the present occasion, there could be no question as to *whence* the sound issued. It came from the fang-like teeth of the dwarf, who ground them and gnashed them as he foamed at the mouth, and glared, with an expression of maniacal rage, into the upturned countenance of the king and the seven companions.

'Ah, ha!' said at length the infuriated jester. 'Ah, ha! I begin to see who these people *are*, now!' Here, pretending to scrutinize the king more closely, he held the flambeau to the flaxon coat which enveloped him, and which instantly burst into a sheet of vivid flame. In less than half a minute the whole eight ourang-outangs were blazing fiercely, amid the shrieks of the multitude who gazed at them from below, horror-stricken, and without the power to render them the slightest assistance.

At length the flames, suddenly increasing in virulence, forced the jester to climb higher up the chain, to be out of their reach; and, as he made this movement, the crowd again sank, for a brief instant, into silence. The dwarf seized his opportunity, and once more spoke:

'I now see *distinctly*,' he said, 'what manner of people these maskers are. They are a great king and his seven privy-councillors – a king who does not scruple to strike a defenceless girl, and his seven councillors who abet him in the outrage. As for myself, I am simply Hop-Frog, the jester – and *this is my last jest*.'

Owing to the high combustibility of both the flax and the tar to which it adhered, the dwarf had scarcely made an end of his brief speech before the work of vengeance was complete. The eight corpses swung in their chains, a fetid, blackened, hideous, and indistinguishable mass. The cripple hurled his torch at them, clambered leisurely to the ceiling, and disappeared through the sky-light.

It is supposed that Trippetta, stationed on the roof of the saloon, had been the accomplice of her friend in his fiery revenge, and that, together, they effected their escape to their own country: for neither was seen again.

Charlotte Brontë 1816–1855

Charlotte Brontë was the eldest surviving daughter of a Yorkshire curate. Born in 1816, she lived to the age of 39; her younger sisters, Emily and Anne, and her brother Branwell all died some years before her. She was from a close-knit family who were interested in religion, politics and the arts.

The Brontë children spent many hours together writing and illustrating their own miniature books about imaginary kingdoms called Angria and Gondal. These stories, many of which survive today, illustrate the issues and characters that interested the young Brontës – the Emperor Napoleon was a particular favourite of Charlotte's and in her teenage years she wrote swashbuckling stories of his adventures. *Napoleon and the Spectre*, written when she was 17, is an example of her early work – a dramatic ghost story which hints, perhaps, at something hidden in Napoleon's past.

As children of a curate, the Brontës had some social standing in their community, but the four children had to work for their living. Bramwell worked as a railway clerk after he had failed to make a success of his chosen career as an artist. Charlotte and her sisters worked away from home as governesses teaching suitable accomplishments to the daughters of wealthy land-owning families. Charlotte, Emily and Anne all hated this work which they found unrewarding and difficult socially. Charlotte explores this role in her most famous novel, *Jane Eyre*, which is the story of the relationship between a governess and her employer. Her other novels also draw on her past life experiences and interests. *Shirley* reflects her political interest in the growth of factories in Victorian Britain; *Villette* and *The Professor* (her first novel, published only after her death), draw upon time she spent studying in Brussels.

Charlotte, Emily and Anne Brontë lived at a time when prejudice against women writers made it difficult for them to have their books accepted for publication. Like George Eliot, they adopted male pseudonyms; their early work was published under the names of Currer, Ellis and Acton Bell. Charlotte was the only one of the sisters to gain recognition and appreciation of her work during her lifetime. She died in 1855, one year after marrying.

Napoleon and the Spectre

Charlotte Brontë

Well, as I was saying, the Emperor got into bed.

'Chevalier,' says he to his valet, 'let down those window-curtains, and shut the casement before you leave the room.'

Chevalier did as he was told, and then, taking up his candlestick, departed.

In a few minutes the Emperor felt his pillow becoming rather hard, and he got up to shake it. As he did so a slight rustling noise was heard near the bed-head. His Majesty listened, but all was silent as he lay down again.

Scarcely had he settled into a peaceful attitude of repose, when he was disturbed by a sensation of thirst. Lifting himself on his elbow, he took a glass of lemonade from the small stand which was placed beside him. He refreshed himself by a deep draught. As he returned the goblet to its station a deep groan burst from a kind of closet in one corner of the apartment.

'Who's there?' cried the Emperor, seizing his pistols. 'Speak, or I'll blow your brains out.'

This threat produced no other effect than a short, sharp laugh, and a dead silence followed.

The Emperor started from his couch, and, hastily throwing on a *robe-de-chambre* which hung over the back of a chair, stepped courageously to the haunted closet. As he opened the door something rustled. He sprang forward sword in hand. No soul or even substance appeared, and the rustling, it was evident, proceeded from the falling of a cloak, which had been suspended by a peg from the door.

Half ashamed of himself he returned to bed.

Just as he was about once more to close his eyes, the light of the three wax tapers, which burned in a silver branch over the mantelpiece, was suddenly darkened. He looked up. A black, opaque shadow obscured it. Sweating with terror, the Emperor put out his hand to seize the bell-rope, but some invisible being snatched it rudely from his grasp, and at the same instant the ominous shade vanished.

'Pooh!' exclaimed Napoleon, 'it was but an ocular delusion.'

'Was it?' whispered a hollow voice, in deep mysterious tones, close to his ear. 'Was it a delusion, Emperor of France? No! all thou hast heard and seen is sad forewarning reality. Rise, lifter of the Eagle Standard! Awake, swayer of the Lily Sceptre! Follow me, Napoleon, and thou shalt see more.'

As the voice ceased, a form dawned on his astonished sight. It was that of a tall, thin man, dressed in a blue surtout* edged with gold lace. It wore a black cravat very tightly round its neck, and confined by two little sticks placed behind each ear. The countenance was livid; the tongue protruded from between the teeth, and the eyes all glazed and bloodshot started with frightful prominence from their sockets.

'*Mon Dieu!*' exclaimed the Emperor, 'what do I see? Spectre, whence cometh thou?'

The apparition spoke not, but gliding forward beckoned Napoleon with uplifted finger to follow.

Controlled by a mysterious influence, which deprived him of the capability of either thinking or acting for himself, he obeyed in silence.

The solid wall of the apartment fell open as they approached, and, when both had passed through, it closed behind them with a noise like thunder.

They would now have been in total darkness had it not been for a dim light which shone round the ghost and revealed the damp walls of a long, vaulted passage. Down this they proceeded with mute rapidity. Ere long a cool, refreshing breeze, which rushed wailing up the vault and caused the Emperor to wrap his loose nightdress closer round, announced their approach to the open air.

* overcoat

This they soon reached, and Nap found himself in one of the principal streets of Paris.

'Worthy Spirit,' said he shivering in the chill night air, 'permit me to return and put on some additional clothing. I will be with you again presently.'

'Forward,' replied his companion sternly.

He felt compelled, in spite of the rising indignation which almost choked him, to obey.

On they went through the deserted streets till they arrived at a lofty house built on the banks of the Seine. Here the Spectre stopped, the gates rolled back to receive them, and they entered a large marble hall which was partly concealed by a curtain drawn across, through the half transparent folds of which a bright light might be seen burning with dazzling lustre. A row of fine female figures, richly attired, stood before this screen. They wore on their heads garlands of the most beautiful flowers, but their faces were concealed by ghastly masks representing death's-heads.

'What is all this mummery?' cried the Emperor, making an effort to shake off the mental shackles by which he was so unwillingly restrained, 'Where am I, and why have I been brought here?'

'Silence,' said the guide, lolling out still further his black and bloody tongue. 'Silence, if thou wouldst escape instant death.'

The Emperor would have replied, his natural courage overcoming the temporary awe to which he had at first been subjected, but just then a strain of wild, supernatural music swelled behind the huge curtain, which waved to and fro, and bellied slowly out as if agitated by some internal commotion or battle of waving winds. At the same moment an over-powering mixture of the scents of mortal corruption, blent with the richest Eastern odours, stole through the haunted hall.

A murmur of many voices was now heard at a distance, and something grasped his arm eagerly from behind.

He turned hastily round. His eyes met the well-known countenance of Marie Louise.

'What! are you in this infernal place, too?' said he. 'What has brought you here?'

'Will your Majesty permit me to ask the same question of yourself?' said the Empress, smiling.

He made no reply; astonishment prevented him.

No curtain now intervened between him and the light. It had been removed as if by magic, and a splendid chandelier appeared suspended over his head. Throngs of ladies, richly dressed, but without death's-head masks, stood round, and a due proportion of gay cavaliers was mingled with them. Music was still sounding, but it was seen to proceed from a band of mortal musicians stationed in an orchestra near at hand. The air was yet redolent of incense, but it was incense unblended with stench.

'*Mon Dieu!*' cried the Emperor, 'how is all this come about? Where in the world is Piche!'

'Piche?' replied the Empress. 'What does your Majesty mean? Had you not better leave the apartment and retire to rest?'

'Leave the apartment? Why, where am I?'

'In my private drawing-room, surrounded by a few particular persons of the Court whom I had invited this evening to a ball. You entered a few minutes since in your nightdress with your eyes fixed and wide open. I suppose from the astonishment you now testify that you are walking in your sleep.'

The Emperor immediately fell into a fit of catalepsy, in which he continued during the whole of that night and the greater part of the next day.

Ambrose Bierce 1842–1914

Ambrose Bierce was born in Ohio in 1842, the tenth child of a farming family. He described his Calvinist upbringing as poor, pinched and mean. At 17 he became a student at the Kentucky Military Institute; during the Civil War he fought as an infantryman, and later as an officer, on the Union side.

In 1866 he settled in San Francisco and began a career in journalism. Apart from three years spent in England and a few months gold mining, Bierce worked as journalist in San Francisco and Washington all of his life. He was famous for the fierce and vitriolic attacks he made through his columns, and was widely known as 'Bitter Bierce'.

He experienced a lot of unhappiness in his personal life; he and his wife separated in 1888; his elder son committed murder and suicide at the age of 16; his younger son died of pneumonia, aggravated by alcoholism, at the age of 27. Like his journalism his short stories are bitter, and often gruesome. Many of the stories are about death and bloodshed; several deal particularly with disposing of unwanted parents in horrible ways. (He grouped four of his stories together under the title 'The Parenticide Club'.) *An Arrest* is typical of Bierce's work in its approach, subject matter and brevity.

In 1914, aged 71, Bierce disappeared while travelling in Mexico during a time of revolutionary war. He was never seen again. He left a final note for his niece: 'Civilization be dinged! – it is the mountains and the desert for me . . . I don't know where I shall be next. Guess it doesn't matter much. Adios, Ambrose.'

An Arrest

Ambrose Bierce

Having murdered his brother-in-law, Orrin Brower of Kentucky was a fugitive from justice. From the county jail where he had been confined to await his trial he had escaped by knocking down his jailer with an iron bar, robbing him of his keys and, opening the outer door, walking out into the night. The jailer being unarmed, Brower got no weapon with which to defend his recovered liberty. As soon as he was out of the town he had the folly to enter a forest; this was many years ago, when that region was wilder than it is now.

The night was pretty dark, with neither moon nor stars visible, and as Brower had never dwelt thereabout, and knew nothing of the lay of the land, he was, naturally, not long in losing himself. He could not have said if he were getting farther away from the town or going back to it – a most important matter to Orrin Brower. He knew that in either case a posse of citizens with a pack of bloodhounds would soon be on his track and his chance of escape was very slender; but he did not wish to assist in his own pursuit. Even an added hour of freedom was worth having.

Suddenly he emerged from the forest into an old road, and there before him saw, indistinctly, the figure of a man, motionless in the gloom. It was too late to retreat: the fugitive felt that at the first movement back toward the wood he would be, as he afterward explained, 'filled with buckshot'. So the two stood there like trees, Brower nearly suffocated by the activity of his own heart; the other – the emotions of the other are not recorded.

A moment later – it may have been an hour – the moon sailed into a patch of unclouded sky and the hunted man saw the visible embodiment of Law lift an arm and point significantly toward and beyond him. He understood. Turning his back to his captor, he walked submissively away in the direction indicated, looking to neither the right nor the left; hardly daring to breathe, his head and back actually aching with a prophecy of buckshot.

Brower was as courageous a criminal as ever lived to be hanged; that was shown by the conditions of awful personal peril in which he had coolly killed his brother-in-law. It is needless to relate them here; they came out at his trial, and the revelation of his calmness in confronting them came near to saving his neck. But what would you have – when a brave man is beaten, he submits.

So they pursued their journey jailward along the old road through the woods. Only once did Brower venture a turn of the head: just once, when he was in deep shadow and he knew that the other was in moonlight, he looked backward. His captor was Burton Duff, the jailer, as white as death and bearing upon his brow the livid mark of the iron bar. Orrin Brower had no further curiosity.

Eventually they entered the town, which was all alight, but deserted; only the women and children remained, and they were off the streets. Straight toward the jail the criminal held his way. Straight up to the main entrance he walked, laid his hand upon the knob of the heavy iron door, pushed it open without command, entered and found himself in the presence of a half-dozen armed men. Then he turned. Nobody else entered.

On a table in the corridor lay the dead body of Burton Duff.

Sir Arthur Conan Doyle 1859–1930

Sherlock Holmes, the great detective, has become one of the best known characters in British fiction. For over a century now, readers have enjoyed stories of Holmes's amazing abilities to solve crimes by the process of careful observation and logical deduction. Through films and television, as well as the original written stories, readers and viewers have become familiar with Sherlock Holmes's long grey travelling cape and deer-stalker hat, his home at 221B Baker Street which he shares with his friend Dr Watson, his love of the violin, of late breakfasts and of smoking tobacco whilst lounging in a blue silk dressing gown, his taste for fencing, Turkish Baths, the Daily Telegraph and for occasional pistol practice in the sitting room . . .

Holmes was first created by Arthur Conan Doyle in a story called *A Study in Scarlet*, published in the 1887 edition of *Beeton's Christmas Annual*. Conan Doyle worked as a doctor at that time; he based the Sherlock Holmes character on Joseph Bell, a surgeon whose logic and powers of observation he admired during his medical training in Edinburgh. The Sherlock Holmes stories soon became very popular with the reading public; six were published in *The Strand* magazine, and in 1891 Conan Doyle gave up his job as a doctor to become a professional writer. By this time, however, he was growing rather tired of the Holmes stories. When the editor of *The Strand* approached him to write another six adventures he agreed only when tempted with the then enormous fee of £50 per story. The first twelve stories were published as a book in 1892. *The Adventure of the Speckled Band*, widely admired as one of the best written and most exciting Sherlock Holmes stories, was in this collection. In 1893 Conan Doyle decided to cut short the famous detective's career; he wrote *The Final Problem* which ends with Holmes and his sworn enemy Moriarty locked in a deadly embrace as they fall together into the swirling torrent below the Reichenbach falls.

Conan Doyle's readers were furious. A letter from one of them began 'You brute!' In 1901 Conan Doyle wrote

The Hound of the Baskervilles presenting it as one of Holmes's 'earlier' adventures. In 1903 he was persuaded to explain (in *The Empty House*) how Holmes had miraculously escaped from his duel with Mariarty. His readers were delighted: staff at railway station bookstalls reported long queues of people eager to buy the magazine that contained the story. Conan Doyle went on to publish three more collections of Holmes stories. His readers were delighted.

He led an active life right up until his death in 1930. He travelled widely, stood twice as a parliamentary candidate for the Liberal party and, after losing his son in the First World War, devoted his time, energy and much of his money to arguing the case for Spiritualism and psychical research.

The Adventure of the Speckled Band

Sir Arthur Conan Doyle

On glancing over my notes of the seventy odd cases in which I have during the last eight years studied the methods of my friend Sherlock Holmes, I find many tragic, some comic, a large number merely strange, but none commonplace; for, working as he did rather for the love of his art than for the acquirement of wealth, he refused to associate himself with any investigation which did not tend towards the unusual, and even the fantastic. Of all these varied cases, however, I cannot recall any which presented more singular features than that which was associated with the well-known Surrey family of the Roylotts of Stoke Moran. The events in question occurred in the early days of my association with Holmes, when we were sharing rooms as bachelors in Baker Street. It is possible that I might have placed them upon record before, but a promise of secrecy was made at the time, from which I have only been freed during the last month by the untimely death of the lady to whom the pledge was given. It is perhaps as well that the facts should now come to light, for I have reasons to know that there are widespread rumours as to the death of Dr Grimesby Roylott which tend to make the matter even more terrible than the truth.

It was early in April in the year '83 that I woke one morning to find Sherlock Holmes standing, fully dressed, by the side of the bed. He was a late riser, as a rule, and as the clock on the mantelpiece showed me that it was only a quarter-past seven, I blinked up at him in some surprise, and perhaps just a little resentment, for I was myself regular in my habits.

'Very sorry to knock you up, Watson,' said he, 'but it's

the common lot this morning. Mrs Hudson has been knocked up, she retorted upon me, and I on you.

'What is it, then – a fire?'

'No; a client. It seems that a young lady has arrived in a considerable state of excitement, who insists upon seeing me. She is waiting now in the sitting-room. Now, when young ladies wander about the metropolis at this hour of the morning, and knock sleepy people up out of their beds, I presume that it is something very pressing which they have to communicate. Should it prove to be an interesting case, you would, I am sure, wish to follow it from the outset. I thought, at any rate, that I should call you and give you the chance.'

'My dear fellow, I would not miss it for anything.'

I had no keener pleasure than in following Holmes in his professional investigations, and in admiring the rapid deductions, as swift as intuitions, and yet always founded on a logical basis, with which he unravelled the problems which were submitted to him. I rapidly threw on my clothes and was ready in a few minutes to accompany my friend down to the sitting-room. A lady dressed in black and heavily veiled, who had been sitting in the window, rose as we entered.

'Good-morning, madam,' said Holmes cheerily. 'My name is Sherlock Holmes. This is my intimate friend and associate, Dr Watson, before whom you can speak as freely as before myself. Ha! I am glad to see that Mrs Hudson has had the good sense to light the fire. Pray draw up to it, and I shall order you a cup of hot coffee, for I observe that you are shivering.'

'It is not cold which makes me shiver,' said the woman in a low voice, changing her seat as requested.

'What, then?'

'It is fear, Mr Holmes. It is terror.' She raised her veil as she spoke, and we could see that she was indeed in a pitiable state of agitation, her face all drawn and gray, with restless, frightened eyes, like those of some hunted animal. Her features and figure were those of a woman of thirty, but her hair was short with premature gray, and her expression was weary and haggard. Sherlock Holmes ran her over with one of his quick, all-comprehensive glances.

'You must not fear,' said he soothingly, bending forward and patting her forearm. 'We shall soon set matters right, I have no doubt. You have come in by train this morning, I see.'

'You know me, then?'

'No, but I observe the second half of a return ticket in the palm of your left glove. You must have started early, and yet you had a good drive in a dog-cart, along heavy roads, before you reached the station.'

The lady gave a violent start and stared in bewilderment at my companion.

'There is no mystery, my dear madam,' said he, smiling. 'The left arm of your jacket is spattered with mud in no less than seven places. The marks are perfectly fresh. There is no vehicle save a dog-cart* which throws up mud in that way, and then only when you sit on the left-hand side of the driver.'

'Whatever your reasons may be, you are perfectly correct,' said she. 'I started from home before six, reached Leatherhead at twenty past, and came in by the first train to Waterloo. Sir, I can stand this strain no longer; I shall go mad if it continues. I have no one to turn to – none, save only one, who cares for me, and he, poor fellow, can be of little aid. I have heard of you, Mr Holmes; I have heard of you from Mrs Farintosh, whom you helped in the hour of her sore need. It was from her that I had your address. Oh, sir, do you not think that you could help me, too, and at least throw a little light through the dense darkness which surrounds me? At present it is out of my power to reward you for your services, but in a month or six weeks I shall be married, with the control of my own income, and then at least you shall not find me ungrateful.'

Holmes turned to his desk and, unlocking it, drew out a small casebook, which he consulted.

'Farintosh,' said he. 'Ah yes, I recall the case; it was concerned with an opal tiara. I think it was before your time, Watson. I can only say, madam, that I shall be happy

* a two-wheeled horse-drawn vehicle.

to devote the same care to your case as I did to that of your friend. As to reward, my profession is its own reward; but you are at liberty to defray whatever expenses I may be put to, at the time which suits you best. And now I beg that you will lay before us everything that may help us in forming an opinion upon the matter.'

'Alas!' replied our visitor, 'the very horror of my situation lies in the fact that my fears are so vague, and my suspicions depend so entirely upon small points, which might seem trivial to another, that even he to whom of all others I have right to look for help and advice looks upon all that I tell him about it as the fancies of a nervous woman. He does not say so, but I can read it from his soothing answers and averted eyes. But I have heard, Mr Holmes, that you can see deeply into the manifold wickedness of the human heart. You may advise me how to walk amid the dangers which encompass me.'

'I am all attention, madam.'

'My name is Helen Stoner, and I am living with my stepfather, who is the last survivor of one of the oldest Saxon families in England, the Roylotts of Stoke Moran, on the western border of Surrey.'

Holmes nodded his head. 'The name is familiar to me.' said he.

'The family was at one time among the richest in England, and the estates extended over the borders into Berkshire in the north, and Hampshire in the west. In the last century, however, four successive heirs were of a dissolute and wasteful disposition, and the family ruin was eventually completed by a gambler in the days of the Regency. Nothing was left save a few acres of ground, and the two-hundred-year-old house, which is itself crushed under a heavy mortgage. The last squire dragged out his existence there, living the horrible life of an aristocratic pauper, but his only son, my stepfather, seeing that he must adapt himself to the new conditions, obtained an advance from a relative, which enabled him to take a medical degree and went out to Calcutta, where, by his professional skill and his force of character, he established a large practice. In a fit of anger, however, caused by some robberies which had been perpetrated in the house, he beat his native butler to death and narrowly escaped a capital sentence. As it was, he suffered a long term of imprisonment and afterwards returned to England a morose and disappointed man.

'When Dr Roylott was in India he married my mother, Mrs Stoner, the young widow of Major-General Stoner, of the Bengal Artillery. My sister Julia and I were twins, and we were only two years old at the time of my mother's remarriage. She had a considerable sum of money – not less than £1000 a year – and this she bequeathed to Dr Roylott entirely while we resided with him, with a provision that a certain annual sum should be allowed to each of us in the event of our marriage. Shortly after our return to England my mother died – she was killed eight years ago in a railway accident near Crewe. Dr Roylott then abandoned his attempts to establish himself in practice in London and took us to live with him in the old ancestral house at Stoke Moran. The money which my mother had left was enough for all our wants, and there seemed to be no obstacle to our happiness.

'But a terrible change came over our stepfather about this time. Instead of making friends and exchanging visits with our neighbours, who had at first been overjoyed to see a Roylott of Stoke Moran back in the old family seat, he shut himself up in his house and seldom came out save to indulge in ferocious quarrels with whoever might cross his path. Violence of temper approaching to mania had been hereditary in the men of the family, and in my stepfather's case it had, I believe, been intensified by his long residence in the tropics. A series of disgraceful brawls took place, two of which ended in the police-court, until at last he became the terror of the village, and the folks would fly at his approach, for he is a man of immense strength, and absolutely uncontrollable in his anger.

'Last week he hurled the local blacksmith over a parapet into a stream, and it was only by paying over all the money which I could gather together that I was able to avert another public exposure. He had no friends at all save the wandering gypsies, and he would give these vagabonds leave to encamp upon the few acres of bramble-covered land which represent the family estate, and would accept in return the hospitality of their tents, wandering away with them sometimes for weeks on end. He has a passion also for Indian animals, which are sent over to him by a correspondent, and he has at this moment a cheetah and a baboon, which wander freely over his grounds and are feared by the villagers almost as much as their master.

'You can imagine from what I say that my poor sister Julia and I had no great pleasure in our lives. No servant would stay with us, and for a long time we did all the work of the house. She was but thirty at the time of her death, and yet her hair had already begun to whiten, even as mine has.'

'Your sister is dead, then?'

'She died just two years ago, and it is of her death that I wish to speak to you. You can understand that, living the life which I have described, we were little likely to see anyone of our own age and position. We had, however, an aunt, my mother's maiden sister, Miss Honoria Westphail, who lives near Harrow, and we were occasionally allowed to pay short visits at this lady's house. Julia went there at Christmas two years ago, and met there a half-pay major of marines, to whom she became engaged. My stepfather learned of the engagement when my sister returned and offered no objection to the marriage; but within a fortnight of the day which had been fixed for the wedding, the terrible event occurred which has deprived me of my only companion.'

Sherlock Holmes had been leaning back in his chair with his eyes closed and his head sunk in a cushion, but he half opened his lids now and glanced across at his visitor.

'Pray be precise as to details,' said he.

'It is easy for me to be so, for every event of that dreadful time is seared into my memory. The manor-house is, as I have already said, very old, and only one wing is now inhabited. The bedrooms in this wing are on the ground floor, the sitting-rooms being in the central block of the buildings. Of these bedrooms the first is Dr Roylott's, the second my sister's, and the third my own. There is no communication between them, but they all open out into the same corridor. Do I make myself plain?'

'Perfectly so.'

'The windows of the three rooms open out upon the lawn. That fatal night Dr Roylott had gone to his room early, though we knew that he had not retired to rest, for my sister was troubled by the smell of the strong Indian cigars which it was his custom to smoke. She left her room, therefore, and came into mine, where she sat for some time, chatting about her approaching wedding. At eleven o'clock she rose to leave me, but she paused at the door and looked back.

'Tell me, Helen,' said she, 'have you ever heard anyone whistle in the dead of the night?'

'Never,' said I.

'I suppose that you could not possibly whistle, yourself, in your sleep?'

'Certainly not. But why?'

'Because during the last few nights I have always, about three in the morning, heard a low, clear whistle. I am a light sleeper, and it has awakened me. I cannot tell where it came from – perhaps from the next room, perhaps from the lawn. I thought that I would just ask you whether you had heard it.'

'No, I have not. It must be those wretched gypsies in the plantation.'

'Very likely. And yet if it were on the lawn, I wonder that you did not hear it also.'

'Ah, but I sleep more heavily than you.'

'Well, it is of no great consequence, at any rate.' She smiled back at me, closed my door, and a few moments later I heard her key turn in the lock.'

'Indeed,' said Holmes. 'Was it your custom always to lock yourselves in at night?'

'Always.'

'And why?'

'I think that I mentioned to you that the doctor kept a cheetah and a baboon. We had no feeling of security unless our doors were locked.'

'Quite so. Pray proceed with your statement.'

'I could not sleep that night. A vague feeling of impending misfortune impressed me. My sister and I, you will recollect, were twins, and you know how subtle are the links which bind two souls which are so closely allied. It was a wild night. The wind was howling outside, and the rain was beating and splashing against the windows. Suddenly, amid all the hubbub of the gale, there burst forth the wild scream of a terrified woman. I knew that it was my sister's voice. I sprang from my bed, wrapped a shawl round me, and rushed into the corridor. As I opened my door I seemed to hear a low whistle, such as my sister described, and a few moments later a clanging sound, as if a mass of metal had fallen. As I ran down the passage, my sister's door was unlocked, and revolved slowly upon its hinges. I stared at it horror-stricken, not knowing what was about to issue from it. By the light of the corridor-lamp I saw my sister appear at the opening, her face blanched with terror, her hands groping for help, her whole figure swaying to and fro like that of a drunkard. I ran to her and threw my arms round her, but at that moment her knees seemed to give way and she fell to the ground. She writhed as one who is in terrible pain, and her limbs were dreadfully convulsed. As first I thought that she had not recognized me, but as I bent over her she suddenly shrieked out in a voice which I shall never forget, 'Oh, my God! Helen! It was the band! The speckled band!' There was something else which she would fain have said, and she stabbed with her finger into the air in the direction of the doctor's room, but a fresh convulsion seized her and choked her words. I rushed out, calling loudly for my stepfather, and I met him hastening from his room in his dressing-gown. When he reached my sister's side she was unconscious, and though he poured brandy down her throat and sent for medical aid from the village, all efforts were in vain, for she slowly sank and died without having recovered her consciousness. Such was the dreadful end of my beloved sister.'

'One moment,' said Holmes; 'are you sure about this whistle and metallic sound? Could you swear to it?'

'That was what the county coroner asked me at the inquiry. It is my strong impression that I heard it, and yet, among the crash of the gale and the creaking of an old house, I may possibly have been deceived.'

'Was your sister dressed?'

'No, she was in her night-dress. In her right hand was found the charred stump of a match, and in her left a match-box.'

'Showing that she had struck a light and looked about her when the alarm took place. That is important. And what conclusions did the coroner come to?'

'He investigated the case with great care, for Dr Roylott's conduct had long been notorious in the county, but he was unable to find any satisfactory cause of death. My evidence showed that the door had been fastened upon the inner side, and the windows were blocked by old-fashioned shutters with broad iron bars, which were secured every night. The walls were carefully sounded, and were shown to be quite solid all round, and the flooring was also thoroughly examined, with the same result. The chimney is wide, but is barred up by four large staples. It is certain, therefore, that my sister was quite alone when she met her end. Besides, there were no marks of any violence upon her.'

'How about poison?'

'The doctors examined her for it, but without success.'

'What do you think that this unfortunate lady died of, then?'

'It is my belief that she died of pure fear and nervous shock, though what it was that frightened her I cannot imagine.'

'Were there gypsies in the plantation at the time?'

'Yes, there are nearly always some there.'

'Ah, and what did you gather from this allusion to a band – a speckled band?'

'Sometimes I have thought that it was merely the wild talk of delirium, sometimes that it may have referred to some band of people, perhaps to these very gypsies in the plantation. I do not know whether the spotted handkerchiefs which so many of them wear over their heads might have suggested the strange adjective which she used.'

Holmes shook his head like a man who is far from being satisfied.

'These are very deep waters,' said he; 'pray go on with your narrative.'

'Two years have passed since then, and my life has been until lately lonelier than ever. A month ago, however, a dear friend, whom I have known for many years, has done me the honour to ask my hand in marriage. His name is Armitage – Percy Armitage – the second son of Mr Armitage, of Crane Water, near Reading. My stepfather has offered no opposition to the match, and we are to be married in the course of the spring. Two days ago some repairs were started in the west wing of the building, and my bedroom wall has been pierced, so that I have had to move into the chamber in which my sister died, and to sleep in the very bed in which she slept. Imagine, then, my thrill of terror when last night, as I lay awake, thinking over her terrible fate, I suddenly heard in the silence of the night the low whistle which had been the herald of her own death. I sprang up and lit the lamp, but nothing was to be seen in the room. I was too shaken to go to bed again, however, so I dressed, and as soon as it was daylight I slipped down, got a dog-cart at the Crown Inn, which is opposite, and drove to Leatherhead, from whence I have come on this morning with the one object of seeing you and asking your advice.'

'You have done wisely,' said my friend. 'But have you told me all?'

'Yes, all.'

'Miss Roylott, you have not. You are screening your stepfather.'

'Why, what do you mean?'

For answer Holmes pushed back the frill of black lace which fringed the hand that lay upon our visitor's knee. Five little livid spots, the marks of four fingers and a thumb, were printed upon the white wrist.

'You have been cruelly used,' said Holmes.

The lady coloured deeply and covered over her injured wrist. 'He is a hard man,' she said, 'and perhaps he hardly knows his own strength.'

There was a long silence, during which Holmes leaned his chin upon his hands and stared into the crackling fires.

'This is a very deep business,' he said at last. 'There are

a thousand details which I should desire to know before I decide upon our course of action. Yet we have not a moment to lose. If we were to come to Stoke Moran to-day, would it be possible for us to see over these rooms without the knowledge of your stepfather?'

'As it happens, he spoke of coming into town to-day upon some most important business. It is probable that he will be away all day, and that there would be nothing to disturb you. We have a housekeeper now, but she is old and foolish, and I could easily get her out of the way.'

'Excellent. You are not averse to this trip, Watson?'

'By no means.'

'Then we shall both come. What are you going to do yourself?'

'I have one or two things which I would wish to do now that I am in town. But I shall return by the twelve o'clock train, so as to be there in time for your coming.'

'And you may expect us early in the afternoon. I have myself some small business matters to attend to. Will you not wait and breakfast?'

'No, I must go. My heart is lightened already since I have confided my trouble to you. I shall look forward to seeing you again this afternoon.' She dropped her thick black veil over her face and glided from the room.

'And what do you think of it all, Watson?' asked Sherlock Holmes, leaning back in his chair.

'It seems to me to be a most dark and sinister business.'

'Dark enough and sinister enough.'

'Yet if the lady is correct in saying that the flooring and walls are sound, and that the door, window, and chimney are impassable, then her sister must have been undoubtedly alone when she met her mysterious end.'

'What becomes, then, of these nocturnal whistles, and what of the very peculiar words of the dying woman?'

'I cannot think.'

'When you combine the ideas of whistles at night, the presence of a band of gypsies who are on intimate terms with this old doctor, the fact that we have every reason to believe that the doctor has an interest in preventing his stepdaughter's marriage, the dying allusion to a band, and, finally, the fact that Miss Helen Stoner heard a metallic clang, which might have been caused by one of those metal bars that secured the shutters falling back into its place, I think that there is good ground to think that the mystery may be cleared along those lines.'

'But what, then, did the gypsies do?'

'I cannot imagine.'

'I see many objections to any such theory.'

'And so do I. It is precisely for that reason that we are going to Stoke Moran this day. I want to see whether the objections are fatal, or if they may be explained away. But what in the name of the devil!'

The ejaculation had been drawn from my companion by the fact that our door had been suddenly dashed open, and that a huge man had framed himself in the aperture. His costume was a peculiar mixture of the professional and of the agricultural, having a black top-hat, a long frockcoat, and a pair of high gaiters, with a hunting-crop swinging in his hand. So tall was he that his hat actually brushed the cross bar of the doorway, and his breadth seemed to span it across from side to side. A large face, seared with a thousand wrinkles, burned yellow with the sun, and marked with every evil passion, was turned from one to the other of us, while his deep-set, bile-shot eyes, and his high, thin, fleshless nose, gave him somewhat the resemblance to a fierce old bird of prey.

'Which of you is Holmes?' asked this apparition.

'My name, sir; but you have the advantage of me,' said my companion quietly.

'I am Dr Grimesby Roylott, of Stoke Moran.'

'Indeed, Doctor,' said Holmes blandly. 'Pray take a seat.'

'I will do nothing of the kind. My stepdaughter has been here. I have traced her. What has she been saying to you?'

'It is a little cold for the time of the year,' said Holmes.

'What has she been saying to you?' screamed the old man furiously.

'But I have heard that the crocuses promise well,' continued my companion imperturbably.

'Ha! You put me off, do you?' said our new visitor, taking a step forward and shaking his hunting-crop. 'I know you, you scoundrel! I have heard of you before. You are Holmes, the meddler.'

My friend smiled.

'Holmes, the busybody!'

His smile broadened.

'Holmes, the Scotland Yard Jack-in-office!'

Holmes chuckled heartily. 'Your conversation is most entertaining.' said he. 'When you go out close the door, for there is a decided draught.'

'I will go when I have said my say. Don't you dare to meddle with my affairs. I know that Miss Stoner has been here. I traced her! I am a dangerous man to fall foul of! See here.' He stepped swiftly forward, seized the poker, and bent it into a curve with his huge brown hands.

'See that you keep yourself out of my grip,' he snarled, and hurling the twisted poker into the fireplace he strode out of the room.

'He seems a very amiable person,' said Holmes, laughing. 'I am not quite so bulky, but if he had remained I might have shown him that my grip was not much more feeble than his own.' As he spoke he picked up the steel poker and, with a sudden effort, straightened it out again.

'Fancy his having the insolence to confound me with the official detective force! This incident gives zest to our investigation, however, and I only trust that our little friend will not suffer from her imprudence in allowing this brute to trace her. And now, Watson, we shall order breakfast, and afterwards I shall walk down to Doctors' Commons, where I hope to get some data which may help us in this matter.'

It was nearly one o'clock when Sherlock Holmes returned from his excursion. He held in his hand a sheet of blue paper, scrawled over with notes and figures.

'I have seen the will of the deceased wife,' said he. 'To determine its exact meaning I have been obliged to work out the present prices of the investments with which it is concerned. The total income, which at the time of the wife's death was little short of £1100, is now, through the fall in agricultural prices, not more than £750. Each daughter can claim an income of £250, in case of marriage. It is evident, therefore, that if both girls had married, this beauty would have had a mere pittance, while even one of them would cripple him to a very serious extent. My morning's work has not been wasted, since it has proved that he had the very strongest motives for standing in the way of anything of the sort. And now, Watson, this is too serious for dawdling, especially as the old man is aware that we are interesting ourselves in his affairs; so if you are ready, we shall call a cab and drive to Waterloo. I should be very much obliged if you would slip your revolver into your pocket. An Eley's No. 2 is an excellent argument with gentlemen who can twist steel poker into knots. That and a toothbrush are, I think, all that we need.'

At Waterloo we were fortunate in catching a train for Leatherhead, where we hired a trap at the station inn and drove for four or five miles through the lovely Surrey lanes. It was a perfect day, with a bright sun and a few fleecy clouds in the heavens. The trees and wayside hedges were just throwing out their first green shoots, and the air was full of the pleasant smell of the moist earth. To me at least there was a strange contrast between the sweet promise of the spring and this sinister quest upon which we were engaged. My companion sat in front of the trap, his arms folded, his hat pulled down over his eyes, and his chin sunk upon his breast, buried in the deepest thought. Suddenly, however, he started, tapped me on the shoulder, and pointed over the meadows.

'Look there!' said he.

A heavily timbered park stretched up in a gentle slope, thickening into a grove at the highest point. From amid the branches there jutted out the gray gables and high roof-tree of a very old mansion.

'Stoke Moran?' said he.

'Yes, sir, that be the house of Dr Grimesby Roylott,' remarked the driver.

'There is some building going on there,' said Holmes; 'that is where we are going.'

'There's the village,' said the driver, pointing to a cluster of roofs some distance to the left; 'but if you want to get to the house, you'll find it shorter to get over this stile, and so by the foot-path over the fields. There it is, where the lady is walking.'

'And the lady, I fancy, is Miss Stoner,' observed Holmes,

shading his eyes. 'Yes, I think we had better do as you suggest.'

We got off, paid our fare, and the trap rattled back on its way to Leatherhead.

'I thought it as well,' said Holmes as we climbed the stile, 'that this fellow should think we had come here as architects, or on some definite business. It may stop his gossip. Good-afternoon, Miss Stoner. You see that we have been as good as our word.'

Our client of the morning had hurried forward to meet us with a face which spoke her joy. 'I have been waiting so eagerly for you,' she cried, shaking hands with us warmly. 'All has turned out splendidly. Dr Roylott has gone to town, and it is unlikely that he will be back before evening.'

'We have had the pleasure of making the doctor's acquaintance,' said Holmes, and in a few words he sketched out what had occurred. Miss Stoner turned white to the lips as she listened.

'Good heavens!' she cried, 'he has followed me, then.'

'So it appears.'

'He is so cunning that I never know when I am safe from him. What will he say when he returns?'

'He must guard himself, for he may find that there is someone more cunning than himself upon his track. You must lock yourself up from him to-night. If he is violent, we shall take you away to your aunt's at Harrow. Now, we must make the best use of our time, so kindly take us at once to the rooms which we are to examine.'

The building was of gray, lichen-blotched stone, with a high central portion and two curving wings, like the claws of a crab, thrown out on each side. In one of these wings the windows were broken and blocked with wooden boards, while the roof was partly caved in, a picture of ruin. The central portion was in a little better repair, but the right-hand block was comparatively modern, and the blinds in the windows, with the blue smoke curling up from the chimneys, showed that this was where the family resided. Some scaffolding had been erected against the end wall, and the stone-work had been broken into, but there were no signs of any workmen at the moment of our visit.

Holmes walked slowly up and down the ill-trimmed lawn and examined with deep attention the outsides of the windows.

'This, I take it, belongs to the room in which you used to sleep, the centre one to your sister's, and the one next to the main building to Dr Roylott's chamber?'

'Exactly so. But I am now sleeping in the middle one.'

'Pending the alterations, as I understand. By the way, there does not seem to be any very pressing need for repairs at that end wall.'

'There were none. I believe that it was an excuse to move me from my room.'

'Ah! that is suggestive. Now, on the other side of this narrow wing runs the corridor from which these rooms open. There are windows in it, of course?'

'Yes, but very small ones. Too narrow for anyone to pass through.'

'As you both locked your doors at night, your rooms were unapproachable from that side. Now, would you have the kindness to go into your room and bar your shutters?'

Miss Stoner did so, and Holmes, after a careful examination through the open window, endeavoured in every way to force the shutter open, but without success. There was no slit through which a knife could be passed to raise the bar. Then with his lens he tested the hinges, but they were of solid iron, built firmly into the massive masonry. 'Hum!' said he, scratching his chin in some perplexity, 'my theory certainly presents some difficulties. No one could pass these shutters if they were bolted. Well, we shall see if the inside throws any light upon the matter.'

A small side door led into the whitewashed corridor from which the three bedrooms opened. Holmes refused to examine the third chamber, so we passed at once to the second, that in which Miss Stoner was now sleeping, and in which her sister had met with her fate. It was a homely little room, with a low ceiling and a gaping fireplace, after the fashion of old country-houses. A brown chest of drawers stood in one corner, a narrow white-counterpaned bed in another, and dressing-table on the left-hand side of the windows. These articles, with two small wickerwork chairs, made up all the furniture in the room save for a square of Wilton carpet in the centre. The boards round and the panelling of the walls were of brown, worm-eaten oak, so old and discoloured that it may have dated from the original building of the house. Holmes drew one of the chairs into a corner and sat silent, while his eyes travelled round and round and up and down, taking in every detail of the apartment.

'Where does that bell communicate with?' he asked at last, pointing to a thick bell-rope which hung down beside the bed, the tassel actually lying upon the pillow.

'It goes to the housekeeper's room.'

'It looks newer than the other things?'

'Yes, it was only put there a couple of years ago.'

'Your sister asked for it, I suppose?'

'No, I never heard of her using it. We used always to get what we wanted for ourselves.'

'Indeed, it seemed unnecessary to put so nice a bell-pull there. You will excuse me for a few minutes while I satisfy myself as to this floor.' He threw himself down upon his face with his lens in his hand and crawled swiftly backward and forward, examining minutely the cracks between the boards. Then he did the same with the wood-work with which the chamber was panelled. Finally he walked over to the bed and spent some time in staring at it and in running his eye up and down the wall. Finally he took the bell-rope in his hand and gave it a brisk tug.

'Why, it's a dummy,' said he.

'Won't it ring?'

'No, it is not even attached to a wire. This is very interesting. You can see now that it is fastened to a hook just above where the little opening for the ventilator is.'

'How very absurd! I never noticed that before.'

'Very strange!' muttered Holmes, pulling at the rope. 'There are one or two very singular points about this room. For example, what a fool a builder must be to open a ventilator into another room, when, with the same trouble, he might have communicated with the outside air!'

'That is also quite modern,' said the lady.

'Done about the same time as the bell-rope?' remarked Holmes.

'Yes, there were several little changes carried out about that time.'

'They seem to have been of a most interesting character – dummy bellropes, and ventilators which do not ventilate. With your permission, Miss Stoner, we shall now carry our researches into the inner apartment.'

Dr Grimesby Roylott's chamber was larger than that of his stepdaughter, but was as plainly furnished. A camp-bed, a small wooden shelf full of books, mostly of a technical character, an armchair beside the bed, a plain wooden chair against the wall, a round table, and a large iron safe were the principal things which met the eye. Holmes walked slowly round and examined each and all of them with the keenest interest.

'What's in here?' he asked, tapping the safe.

'My stepfather's business papers.'

'Oh! you have seen inside, then?'

'Only once, some years ago. I remember that it was full of papers.'

'There isn't a cat in it, for example?'

'No. What a strange idea!'

'Well, look at this!' He took up a small saucer of milk which stood on the top of it.

'No; we don't keep a cat. But there is a cheetah and a baboon.'

'Ah, yes, of course! Well, a cheetah is just a big cat, and yet a saucer of milk does not go very far in satisfying its wants, I daresay. There is one point which I should wish to determine.' He squatted down in front of the wooden chair and examined the seat of it with the greatest attention.

'Thank you. That is quite settled,' said he, rising and putting his lens in his pocket. 'Hello! Here is something interesting!'

The object which had caught his eye was a small dog lash hung on one corner of the bed. The lash, however, was curled upon itself and tied so as to make a loop of whipcord.

'What do you make of that, Watson?'

'It's a common enough lash. But I don't know why it should be tied.'

'That is not quite so common, is it? Ah, me! it's a wicked

world, and when a clever man turns his brains to crime it is the worst of all. I think that I have seen enough now, Miss Stoner, and with your permission we shall walk out upon the lawn.'

I had never seen my friend's face so grim or his brow so dark as it was when we turned from the scene of this investigation. We had walked several times up and down the lawn, neither Miss Stoner nor myself liking to break in upon his thoughts before he roused himself from his reverie.

'It is very essential, Miss Stoner,' said he, 'that you should absolutely follow my advice in every respect.'

'I shall most certainly do so.'

'The matter is too serious for any hesitation. Your life may depend upon your compliance.'

'I assure you that I am in your hands.'

'In the first place, both my friend and I must spend the night in your room.'

Both Miss Stoner and I gazed at him in astonishment.

'Yes, it must be so. Let me explain. I believe that that is the village inn over there?'

'Yes, that is the Crown.'

'Very good. Your windows would be visible from there?'

'Certainly.'

'You must confine yourself to your room, on pretence of a headache, when your stepfather comes back. Then when you hear him retire for the night, you must open the shutters of your window, undo the hasp, put your lamp there as a signal to us, and then withdraw quietly with everything which you are likely to want into the room which you used to occupy. I have no doubt that, in spite of the repairs, you could manage there for one night.'

'Oh, yes, easily.'

'The rest you will leave in our hands.'

'But what will you do?'

'We shall spend the night in your room, and we shall investigate the cause of this noise which has disturbed you.'

'I believe, Mr Holmes, that you have already made up your mind,' said Miss Stoner, laying her hand upon my companion's sleeve.

'Perhaps I have.'

'Then, for pity's sake, tell me what was the cause of my sister's death.'

'I should prefer to have clearer proofs before I speak.'

'You can at least tell me whether my own thought is correct, and if she died from some sudden fright.'

'No, I do not think so. I think that there was probably some more tangible cause. And now, Miss Stoner, we must leave you, for if Dr Roylott returned and saw us our journey would be in vain. Good-bye, and be brave, for if you will do what I have told you you may rest assured that we shall soon drive away the dangers that threaten you.'

Sherlock Holmes and I had no difficulty in engaging a bedroom and sitting-room at the Crown Inn. They were on the upper floor, and from our window we could command a view of the avenue gate, and of the inhabited wing of Stoke Moran Manor House. At dusk we saw Dr Grimesby Roylott drive past, his huge form looming up beside the little figure of the lad who drove him. The boy had some slight difficulty in undoing the heavy iron gates, and we heard the hoarse roar of the doctor's voice and saw the fury with which he shook his clinched fists at him. The trap drove on, and a few minutes later we saw a sudden light spring up among the trees as the lamp was lit in one of the sitting-rooms.

'Do you know, Watson,' said Holmes as we sat together in the gathering darkness, 'I have really some scruples as to taking you to-night. There is a distinct element of danger.'

'Can I be of assistance?'

'Your presence might be invaluable.'

'Then I shall certainly come.'

'It is very kind of you.'

'You speak of danger. You have evidently seen more in these rooms than was visible to me.'

'No, but I fancy that I may have deduced a little more. I imagined that you saw all that I did.'

'I saw nothing remarkable save the bell-rope, and what purpose that could answer I confess is more than I can imagine.'

'You saw the ventilator, too?'

'Yes, but I do not think that it is such a very unusual thing to have a small opening between two rooms. It was so small that a rat could hardly pass through.'

'I knew that we should find a ventilator before ever we came to Stoke Moran.'

'My dear Holmes!'

'Oh, yes, I did. You remember in her statement she said that her sister could smell Dr Roylott's cigar. Now, of course that suggested at once that there must be a communication between the two rooms. It could only be a small one, or it would have been remarked upon at the coroner's inquiry. I deduced a ventilator.'

'But what harm can there be in that?'

'Well, there is at least a curious coincidence of dates. A ventilator is made, a cord is hung, and a lady who sleeps in the bed dies. Does not that strike you?'

'I cannot as yet see any connection.'

'Did you observe anything very peculiar about that bed?'

'No.'

'It was clamped to the floor. Did you ever see a bed fastened like that before?'

'I cannot say that I have.'

'The lady could not move her bed. It must always be in the same relative position to the ventilator and to the rope – or so we may call it, since it was clearly never meant for a bell-pull.'

'Holmes,' I cried, 'I seem to see dimly what you are hinting at. We are only just in time to prevent some subtle and horrible crime.'

'Subtle enough and horrible enough. When a doctor does go wrong he is the first of criminals. He has nerve and he has knowledge. Palmer and Pritchard were among the heads of their profession. This man strikes even deeper, but I think, Watson, that we shall be able to strike deeper still. But we shall have horrors enough before the night is over; for goodness' sake let us have a quiet pipe and turn our minds for a few hours to something more cheerful.'

About nine o'clock the light among the trees was extinguished, and all was dark in the direction of the Manor House. Two hours passed slowly away, and then, suddenly, just at the stroke of eleven, a single bright light shone out right in front of us.

'That is our signal,' said Holmes, springing to his feet; 'it comes from the middle window.'

As we passed out he exchanged a few words with the landlord, explaining that we were going on a late visit to an acquaintance, and that it was possible that we might spend the night there. A moment later we were out on the dark road, a chill wind blowing in our faces, and one yellow light twinkling in front of us through the gloom to guide us on our sombre errand.

There was little difficulty in entering the grounds, for unrepaired breaches gaped in the old park wall. Making our way among the trees, we reached the lawn, crossed it, and were about to enter through the window when out from a clump of laurel bushes there darted what seemed to be a hideous and distorted child, who threw itself upon the grass with writhing limbs and then ran swiftly across the lawn into the darkness.

'My God!' I whispered; 'did you see it?'

Holmes was for the moment as startled as I. His hand closed like a vice upon my wrist in his agitation. Then he broke into a low laugh and put his lips to my ear.

'It is a nice household,' he murmured. 'That is the baboon.'

I had forgotten the strange pets which the doctor affected. There was a cheetah, too; perhaps we might find it upon our shoulders at any moment. I confess that I felt easier in my mind when, after following Holmes's example and slipping off my shoes, I found myself inside the bedroom. My companion noiselessly closed the shutters, moved the lamp onto the table, and cast his eyes round the room. All was as we had seen it in the daytime. Then creeping up to me and making a trumpet of his hand, he whispered into my ear again so gently that it was all that I could do to distinguish the words:

'The least sound would be fatal to our plans.'

I nodded to show that I had heard.

'We must sit without light. He would see it through the ventilator.' I nodded again.

'Do not go asleep; your very life may depend upon it.

Have your pistol ready in case we should need it. I will sit on the side of the bed, and you in that chair.'

I took out my revolver and laid it on the corner of the table.

Holmes had brought up a long thin cane, and this he placed upon the bed beside him. By it he laid the box of matches and the stump of a candle. The he turned down the lamp, and we were left in darkness.

How shall I ever forget that dreadful vigil? I could not hear a sound, not even the drawing of a breath, and yet I knew that my companion sat open-eyed, within a few feet of me, in the same state of nervous tension in which I was myself. The shutters cut off the least ray of light, and we waited in absolute darkness. From outside came the occasional cry of a night-bird, and once at our very window a long drawn catlike whine, which told us that the cheetah was indeed at liberty. Far away we could hear the deep tones of the parish clock, which boomed out every quarter of an hour. How long they seemed, those quarters! Twelve struck, and one and two and three, and still we sat waiting silently for whatever might befall.

Suddenly there was the momentary gleam of a light up in the direction of the ventilator, which vanished immediately, but was succeeded by a strong smell of burning oil and heated metal. Someone in the next room had lit a dark-lantern. I heard a gentle sound of movement, and than all was silent once more, though the smell grew stronger. For half an hour I sat with straining ears. Then suddenly another sound became audible – a very gentle, soothing sound, like that of a small jet of steam escaping continually from a kettle. The instant that we heard it, Holmes sprang from the bed, struck a match, and lashed furiously with his cane at the bell-pull.

'You see it, Watson?' he yelled. 'You see it?'

But I saw nothing. At the moment when Holmes struck the light I heard a low, clear whistle, but the sudden glare flashing into my weary eyes made it impossible for me to tell what it was at which my friend lashed so savagely. I could, however, see that his face was deadly pale and filled with horror and loathing.

He had ceased to strike and was gazing up at the

ventilator when suddenly there broke from the silence of the night the most horrible cry to which I have ever listened. It swelled up louder and louder, a hoarse yell of pain and fear and anger all mingled in the one dreadful shriek. They say that away down in the village, and even in the distant parsonage, that cry raised the sleepers from their beds. It struck cold to our hearts, and I stood gazing at Holmes, and he at me, until the last echoes of it had died away into the silence from which it rose.

'What can it mean?' I gasped.

'It means that it is all over,' Holmes answered. 'And perhaps, after all, it is for the best. Take your pistol, and we will enter Dr Roylott's room.'

With a grave face he lit the lamp and led the way down the corridor. Twice he struck at the chamber door without any reply from within. Then he turned the handle and entered, I at his heels, with the cocked pistol in my hand.

It was a singular sight which met our eyes. On the table stood a dark lantern with the shutter half open, throwing a brilliant beam of light upon the iron safe, the door of which was ajar. Beside this table, on the wooden chair, sat Dr Grimesby Roylott, clad in a long gray dressing-gown, his bare ankles protruding beneath, and his feet thrust into red heelless Turkish slippers. Across his lap lay the short stock with the long lash which we had noticed during the day. His chin was cocked upward and his eyes were fixed in a dreadful, rigid stare at the corner of the ceiling. Round his brow he had a peculiar yellow band, with brownish speckles, which seemed to be bound tightly round his head. As we entered he made neither sound nor motion.

'The band! the speckled band!' whispered Holmes.

I took a step forward. In an instant his strange headgear began to move, and there reared itself from among his hair the squat diamond-shaped head and puffed neck of a loathsome serpent.

'It is a swamp adder!' cried Holmes; 'the deadliest snake in India. He has died within ten seconds of being bitten. Violence does, in truth, recoil upon the violent, and the schemer falls into the pit which he digs for another. Let us thrust this creature back into its den, and we can then remove Miss Stoner to some place of shelter and let the county police know what has happened.'

As he spoke he drew the dog-whip swiftly from the dead man's lap, and throwing the noose round the reptile's neck he drew it from its horrid perch and, carrying it at arm's length, threw it into the iron safe, which he closed upon it.

Such are the true facts of the death of Dr Grimesby Roylott, of Stoke Moran. It is not necessary that I should prolong a narrative which has already run to too great a length by telling how we broke the sad news to the terrified girl, how we conveyed her by the morning train to the care of her good aunt at Harrow, of how the slow process of official inquiry came to the conclusion that the doctor met his fate while indiscreetly playing with a dangerous pet. The little which I had yet to learn of the case was told me by Sherlock Holmes as we travelled back next day.

'I had,' said he, 'come to an entirely erroneous conclusion which shows, my dear Watson, how dangerous it always is to reason from insufficient data. The presence of the gypsies, and the use of the word 'band,' which was used by the poor girl, no doubt to explain the appearance which she had caught a hurried glimpse of by the light of her match, were sufficient to put me upon an entirely wrong scent. I can only claim the merit that I instantly reconsidered my position when, however, it became clear to me that whatever danger threatened an occupant of the room could not come either from the window or the door. My attention was speedily drawn, as I have already remarked to you, to this ventilator, and to the bell-rope which hung down to the bed. The discovery that this was a dummy, and that the bed was clamped to the floor, instantly gave rise to the suspicion that the rope was there as a bridge for something passing through the hole and coming to the bed. The idea of a snake instantly occurred to me, and when I coupled it with my knowledge that the doctor was furnished with a supply of creatures from India, I felt that I was probably on the right track. The idea of using a form of poison which could not possibly be discovered by any chemical test was just such a one as would occur to a clever and ruthless man who had had an Eastern training. The rapidity with which such a poison would take effect would also, from his point of view, be an advantage. It would be a sharp-eyed coroner, indeed, who could distinguish the two little dark punctures which would show where the poison fangs had done their work. Then I thought of the whistle. Of course he must recall the snake before the morning light revealed it to the victim. He had trained it, probably by the use of the milk which we saw, to return to him when summoned. He would put it through this ventilator at the hour that he thought best, with the certainty that it would crawl down the rope and land on the bed. It might or might not bite the occupant, perhaps she might escape every night for a week, but sooner or later she must fall a victim.

'I had come to these conclusions before ever I had entered his room. An inspection of his chair showed me that he had been in the habit of standing on it, which of course would be necessary in order that he should reach the ventilator. The sight of the safe, the saucer of milk, and the loop of whipcord were enough to finally dispel any doubts which may have remained. The metallic clang heard by Miss Stoner was obviously caused by her stepfather hastily closing the door of his safe upon its terrible occupant. Having once made up my mind, you know the steps which I took in order to put the matter to the proof. I heard the creature hiss as I have no doubt that you did also, and I instantly lit the light and attacked it.'

'With the result of driving it through the ventilator.'

'And also with the result of causing it to turn upon its master at the other side. Some of the blows of my cane came home and roused its snakish temper, so that it flew upon the first person it saw. In this way I am no doubt indirectly responsible for Dr Grimesby Roylott's death, and I cannot say that it is likely to weigh very heavily upon my conscience.'

ALSO IN

Founding Editors: Anne and Ian Serraillier

Chinua Achebe Things Fall Apart
David Almond Skellig
Maya Angelou I Know Why the Caged Bird Sings
Margaret Atwood The Handmaid's Tale
Jane Austen Pride and Prejudice
Stan Barstow Joby: A Kind of Loving
Nina Bawden Carrie's War; The Finding; Humbug
Malorie Blackman Tell Me No Lies; Words Last Forever
Charlotte Brontë Jane Eyre
Emily Brontë Wuthering Heights
Melvin Burgess and Lee Hall Billy Elliot
Betsy Byars The Midnight Fox; The Pinballs; The Eighteenth Emergency
Victor Canning The Runaways
Sir Arthur Conan Doyle Sherlock Holmes Short Stories
Susan Cooper King of Shadows
Robert Cormier Heroes
Roald Dahl Danny; The Champion of the World; The Wonderful Story of Henry Sugar; George's Marvellous Medicine; The Witches; Boy; Going Solo; Matilda; My Year
Anita Desai The Village by the Sea
Charles Dickens A Christmas Carol; Great Expectations; A Charles Dickens Selection
Berlie Doherty Granny was a Buffer Girl; Street Child
Roddy Doyle Paddy Clarke Ha Ha Ha
George Eliot Silas Marner
Anne Fine The Granny Project
Leon Garfield Six Shakespeare Stories
Ann Halam Dr Franklin's Island
Thomas Hardy The Withered Arm and Other Wessex Tales; The Mayor of Casterbridge
Ernest Hemmingway The Old Man and the Sea; A Farewell to Arms
Barry Hines A Kestrel For A Knave
Nigel Hinton Buddy; Buddy's Song
Anne Holm I Am David

Janni Howker Badger on the Barge; The Nature of the Beast; Martin Farrell
Pete Johnson The Protectors
Geraldine Kaye Comfort Herself
Daniel Keyes Flowers for Algernon
Dick King-Smith The Sheep-Pig
Elizabeth Laird Red Sky in the Morning
D H Lawrence The Fox and The Virgin and the Gypsy; Selected Tales
Harper Lee To Kill a Mockingbird
C Day Lewis The Otterbury Incident
Joan Linguard Across the Barricades
Penelope Lively The Ghost of Thomas Kemp
Geraldine McCaughrean Stories from Shakespeare; Pack of Lies
Bernard MacLaverty Cal; The Best of Bernard MacLaverty
Jan Mark Heathrow Nights
James Vance Marshall Walkabout
Ian McEwan The Daydreamer; A Child in Time
Michael Morpurgo The Wreck of the Zanzibar; Why the Whales Came; Arthur, High King of Britain; Kensuke's Kingdom; From Hereabout Hill; Robin of Sherwood
Beverley Naidoo No Turning Back; The Other Side of Truth
Bill Naughton The Goalkeeper's Revenge
New Windmill A Charles Dickens Selection
New Windmill Anthology of Challenging Texts: Thoughtlines
New Windmill Book of Classic Short Stories
New Windmill Book of Fiction and Non-fiction: Taking Off!
New Windmill Book of Greek Myths
New Windmill Book of Haunting Tales
New Windmill Book of Humorous Stories: Don't Make Me Laugh
New Windmill Book of Nineteenth Century Short Stories
New Windmill Book of Non-fiction: Get Real
New Windmill Book of Non-fiction: Real Lives, Real Times
New Windmill Book of Scottish Short Stories
New Windmill Book of Short Stories: Fast and Curious
New Windmill Book of Short Stories: From Beginning to End
New Windmill Book of Short Stories: Into the Unknown
New Windmill Book of Short Stories: Tales with a Twist
New Windmill Book of Short Stories: Trouble in Two Centuries
New Windmill Book of Short Stories: Ways with Words
New Windmill Book of Stories from Many Cultures and Traditions; Fifty-Fifty Tuti-Fruity Chocolate Chip

How many have you read?